SPRINKLES AND SEA SERPENTS

A SUGAR SHACK WITCH MYSTERY

DANIELLE GARRETT

ROOTS & WINGS
PRESS

BOOKS BY DANIELLE GARRETT

BEECHWOOD HARBOR MAGIC MYSTERIES

Murder's a Witch

Twice the Witch

Witch Slapped

Witch Way Home

Along Came a Ghost

Lucky Witch

Betwixt: A Beechwood Harbor Collection

One Bad Witch

A Royal Witch

First Place Witch

Sassy Witch

The Witch Is Inn

Men Love Witches

Goodbye's a Witch

BEECHWOOR HARBOR GHOST MYSTERIES

The Ghost Hunter Next Door

Ghosts Gone Wild

When Good Ghosts Get the Blues

Big Ghosts Don't Cry

Diamonds are a Ghost's Best Friend

Ghosts Just Wanna Have Fun

Bad Ghosts Club

Mean Ghosts

SUGAR SHACK WITCH MYSTERIES

Sprinkles and Sea Serpents

Grimoires and Gingerbread

Mermaids and Meringue

Sugar Cookies and Sirens

Hexes and Honey Buns

Leprechauns and Lemon Bars

NINE LIVES MAGIC MYSTERIES

Witchy Whiskers

Hexed Hiss-tory

Cursed Claws

Purr-fect Potions

Furry Fortunes

Talisman Tails

Stray Spells

Mystic Meow

Catnip Charms

Yuletide Yowl

Paw-ful Premonition

Growling Grimoire

MAGIC INN MYSTERIES

Witches in the Kitchen

Fairies in the Foyer

Ghosts in the Garden

HAVEN PARANORMAL ROMANCES

Once Upon a Hallow's Eve

A TOUCH OF MAGIC MYSTERIES

Cupid in a Bottle

Newly Wed and Slightly Dead

Couture and Curses

Wedding Bells and Deadly Spells

CHAPTER ONE

The silver machine stared at me, cold and unfeeling. In that moment, I would have rather taken on a charging, fire-breathing dragon. Doubt furled into a tight ball in the pit of my stomach as I marched myself towards the building. The man in front of me stepped aside, leaving me to face the computerized beast on my own.

Cringing, I stepped nearer and rammed my debit card into the ATM's slot. The machine gave a dull beep, like some kind of mocking tone. Almost as though it were asking, "Are you sure you want to do this?"

I didn't. But I also had no choice. I'd lived in denial for the past week and a half, but now it was time to rejoin the land of reality.

Lucky me.

With bated breath, I squinted at the screen and pressed the Check Balance button.

$28.27.

Muttering a string of curse words, I punched buttons and toggled through the menu. I didn't need to bother checking the savings account. I'd cleaned that out last time I'd braved facing the machine. Another electronic whir and a crisp twenty-dollar bill appeared in the slot under the screen. I shoved it and my debit card back into my wallet, canceled out of the ATM menu, spun on my heel, and stalked across the convenience store parking lot to my 2000 Ford Focus. It was the wagon-style model, painted in a color they called *champagne*, which was a little ridiculous considering it was more of a beer-budget kind of car, especially by the time I'd purchased it. The thing was on its last legs —or pistons or whatever it was that kept the thing going *putt-putt-putt* down the highway.

Car stuff wasn't my forte.

I dropped into the driver's seat and stared out the windshield. In the passenger seat beside me sat a banker's box with an assortment of random items. A potted African violet, pads of rainbow-colored Post-It notes, a couple inspirational postcards I'd kept tacked to my cubicle wall, a few outdated magazines swiped from the break room recycle bin, the ergonomic keyboard and mouse that I'd had to pay for out of my own pocket because the company was too cheap to provide proper equipment for their staff—at least, us underlings. Lastly, a silver photo frame containing a picture of my family, taken what felt like a lifetime ago.

The banker's box was all that remained of my plans. Of my hopes and dreams.

As I sat in the lot and stared at the convenience store, rain splashed down on the windshield. A wry smile twisted my lips. *How fitting.*

I'd pick up my final paycheck on Friday. Until then, the twenty in my pocket was going to have to see me through.

Rumbling out of the lot, I turned right and headed back to my apartment building. The brown siding was old and faded, the flower beds filled with bark dust and only a few stubby remnants of the flowers planted in spring. The place wasn't much to look at, but it fit in my budget and the inside of my one-bedroom unit came with a fresh coat of paint and new laminate floors when I'd signed the lease six months ago. A lease that was set to expire in thirty-two days.

Shoving aside that barely pinned anxiety grenade, I parked in the covered spot designated for my apartment and squeezed out of the door, careful not to ding the SUV beside me. Whoever had painted the lines in the complex's lot must have gone to the same school as whoever was in charge of making airplane seats shrink every year. On more than one occasion I'd been forced to pop my car's hatch and climb out through the rear because there was no way to get the doors open. Luckily, my neighbor on the other side was still at work, so I was able to retrieve the banker's box without much trouble.

Sighing, I swung my hip at the passenger door, slamming it shut, then started for the narrow stairway leading to my unit on the second floor of the two-story complex. It was still raining. I stepped out from under the cover of the parking structure and a gust of wind grabbed at my snow-white hair, flinging it into my face, along with a smattering of fat raindrops. I huffed out three quick breaths, trying to clear my hair from my face, but it was no use. I was in the process of balancing the box on one arm when a male voice cut through the bluster.

"Hey, Ella!"

I blinked a few times and shoved my hair off my wet cheek.

A tall man offered me a crooked smile as he rose from his seat on the second-to-the-last step of the staircase leading to my apartment.

Somewhere in my chest, a knot tightened. "Leo? What are you doing here?"

"Just got back into town, from London, and I was on the plane and I was thinking about—" Leo trailed off as he glanced down and studied the contents of the box. "Ella, is this—did you—"

"Yes!" I snapped before dragging a hand across my face to clear the lingering strands of hair and the rain. I likely smeared my mascara and eyeliner in the process, but I was already running unopposed in the drowned-rat look-alike contest, so what did it matter?

Leo, on the other hand, looked handsome and

4

polished as ever. He stood six feet two inches, with a lean, athletic build. He wasn't super muscular, but he wasn't a beanpole either. He was somewhere in between, with tanned skin that went even deeper in the summer, thanks to his Italian heritage. His dark brown eyes were flecked with gold, and shone even brighter when he smiled—which was almost always.

He wore a pair of designer jeans, with sneakers that had likely cost the same as my rent, with a persimmon-colored sweater under his black jacket. I knew the sweater well. It was the one I'd given him the year before, as a Christmas gift.

"What happened, Ella?" Leo prompted.

"They canned me," I said, wrapping both arms around the box like it was some kind of teddy bear.

"Come on, let's get you out of the rain," Leo said, taking the box from my arm before I could object.

"Leo, I—" My protest died quickly as his warm arm looped around my shoulders and he shepherded me into the covered breezeway between the first-floor units.

He leaned over, put the box on the ground at his feet, and then gathered me in close. That was right about the time the little knot in my chest broke into little pieces like an explosion of super depressing confetti, and a sob escaped.

"Oh, Ella," Leo said, squeezing me tighter. "I'm so sorry. Do you want to talk about it?"

Debating my answer, I blinked away the tears and

realized there was a small carry-on suitcase sitting to the left of the stoop where he'd been sitting. "Leo?" I asked, taking a half step back from the embrace. "What are you *really* doing here?"

Leo turned slightly, following my gaze. A flush of color appeared along his defined cheekbones. "Well, like I said, El, I just got off a plane from London, and I uh—well, I wanted to see you."

My heart sank even lower. "Leo, we said we would stop doing this. It's been over for months. There isn't anything left to talk about."

Leo's signature half-crooked smile returned as his deep brown eyes shifted back to mine. "We could skip the talking part, if you'd prefer."

I laughed, the first honest-to-the-goddess laugh I'd had in weeks. It felt good. Still smiling, I leaned over and retrieved the box of my belongings from the cement walkway. I knew I should tell him to go home, back to his fancy high-rise condo on the other side of town, but the truth was, I didn't want to be alone. I didn't want to spend the night staring at the ceiling, delaying the inevitable. I already knew what was coming next. There weren't any other options.

But that could wait till tomorrow.

"Come on," I said to Leo as I started up the stairs. "I'll at least let you buy me dinner."

My apartment stood in stark contrast to the place Leo and I shared during the majority of our relationship. The place he still called home. It had been my choice to move out. Leo had offered to let me stay in one of the other bedrooms, and I had, for a time, but we both knew that eventually one or both of us was going to want to start dating again, and trying to bring someone new into the situation wasn't going to turn out as cute and clean as in a soapy rom-com.

Our relationship—our engagement—had ended on friendly enough terms. But in some ways that only made it more difficult. Every time we got a little distance from each other, we'd slip right back into pining for the way things used to be, when we were together. Then we'd end up right where we were now, sharing a meal, trying to avoid prolonged eye contact, all the while wondering why we couldn't make it work.

But the truth was, we just couldn't.

Especially with what was coming next. I'd made a decision that would throw ice on the tiny embers of hope for ever making things work with Leo. He just didn't know it yet.

After tonight, everything would change.

"START AT THE BEGINNING," Leo prompted once we'd ordered some delivery Tex-Mex. "Why would they fire you? You're the best beat reporter they've got."

"Well, they don't see it that way." A rueful smile tugged on my lips. "In fact, it's worse than that—they think I'm a plagiarizer."

7

Leo's mouth fell open. He sputtered, trying to find the right words. "But that's—I mean—you—of all—how could they think that?"

"Oh, they had a little help," I replied dryly as I crossed to the fridge. I yanked open the door and almost closed it right away. I didn't want Leo to see how bare it was. There was nothing but a six-pack of hard ciders and a few jars of condiments. Angling my body to block most of it from sight, I grabbed two cans and closed the door again. "You remember that big story I was working on? About the Beaumont family?"

Leo nodded and accepted the can of hard cider. "Sure."

"I submitted it last night to my editor, and this morning, I got called in to speak with her about it." I laughed, the sound hollow. "I actually thought it was going to be to tell me I'd finally be getting the promotion to editor. I'd get my own desk. I'd get to actually *write*, instead of just dig up facts and hand them off to someone else. I thought my years of gofer work had finally paid off."

Leo cast a dark look at the pull tab on the can before cracking it back.

"Instead," I continued, the word pointed, "I was informed that I'd lifted big chunks of the piece from one of the other reporters trying for the editor position."

"*What?*" Leo hissed. "But how is that even possible?"

"Yasmine swiped it from my computer, changed a

few things to fit her style, and submitted it the night before I turned my version in. She's getting the job, based off the work *I* did while she was out downing bottomless mimosas at brunch and refreshing her mani-pedi on the weekends."

"Can't they call and see who submitted the piece? Or, you could show them your revision history on the file on your computer! That would prove you were the author."

"It's all gone," I said. "*Poof.* It's not on my computer, it's not on the cloud. It's just gone. And, since I was keeping it so close to the vest, I hadn't even submitted partial drafts to my editor. I was too proud. I've spent years having every story critiqued and torn to shreds before I even finished the first draft, and I'd finally reached a place where Sabrina trusted me. She left me alone until I had the whole story written." I rubbed my fingers along my forehead, staring at the cabinets lining the wall. "Stupid. Arrogant." I punctuated the words with jabs at my forehead.

"Hey, hey," Leo chided, gently taking my hand away. He clasped both of his around it and kissed the back of my knuckles. "You're not stupid, Ella. And you're far from arrogant. In fact, you're one of the humblest people I know, especially in this business. I spent two years begging you to see your own talent and to stop beating yourself up and comparing your work to people who've been at this for decades."

"It doesn't matter now," I said, shaking my head. My

lips pressed together as I fought back another round of tears. "I'm blackballed. No one will hire me now. My resume is forever marred, and even if I could prove that I wrote that piece, the rumors are going to follow me everywhere I go."

"Come on, babe. This just happened. Let's take a couple days and figure out a plan. We'll call a couple lawyers, you know they have people who can find anything. They'll do their digital-detective thing and get you your job back. Hey, you can probably sue Yasmine for damages! That might be fun. Right?"

My shoulders sagged. "I can't afford a lawyer, Leo."

The image from the ATM screen appeared behind my eyelids when I blinked. I barely had enough to buy a decent combo meal at a fast-food joint. If not for Leo showing up, I'd have spent my evening at the dollar store around the corner, filling a basket with bricks of ramen and bags of stale tortilla chips.

"I'll pay for the lawyer," Leo said. "I can cover it."

I shot him a look. "I can't let you do that, Leo. We're not even together anymore, and it would just—"

A pained look flashed across his face. "What if we were … together?"

"Leo," I groaned, pacing a few feet away before turning back to face him. "I can't do this right now. I can't have this conversation again."

"Ella, I know we've gone through this before, but when I was in London, all I could think about was how you should have been there with me. Just like we always talked about. You could go to a café or book-shop and write, while I was out doing a shoot, and that night, we'd get together at some fancy restaurant and drink and talk about the day—"

I squeezed my eyes closed, trying to block out the images he was painting. We'd been down this road too many times, and it always looped back around to the same destination.

The doorbell rang, announcing our food delivery, and my eyes popped open. Leo's gaze locked on mine for a heart-stopping minute, before he relented and went to get the door. His shoulders sagged slightly as he turned away, and my heart twisted. I didn't want to hurt him. It was the last thing I would ever want to do, but there were things I couldn't tell him. Huge chunks of my life that I had to keep hidden. My family, my past, the way I'd been raised. All of it was locked in secrets and half-truths, forming a huge impenetrable barrier between us.

Sighing, I leaned against the counter. It was over now. I couldn't fall back into Leo's arms and let him carry me away. Not this time. This time I had to go back to the one place I swore I'd never go again.

Next week, I'd load up whatever belongings I couldn't sell off, and I'd make the drive up to Winter-spell Lake.

Back home.

CHAPTER TWO

The following week and a half passed quickly, following my goodbye with Leo. The memory of that final embrace and the single tear on his cheek stuck with me as I packed my things, sold the others, and left Portland. Even with my final paycheck from the paper, I couldn't afford another month's rent, so I'd been forced to let my lease lapse and take the loss. I packed up my Focus, stuffing it to the brim, and headed up the I-5 toward the Oregon-Washington border, then kept going north.

Eventually, I turned onto the highway to the east, and after another hour and a half, took a familiar exit disguised as an emergency turnoff outlet for large trucks. A little way up the gravel road, a sun-bleached road sign welcomed me to Winterspell Lake. I let off the gas pedal and started to slow my speed. With a heavy exhale, I crawled past the sign.

It was official. I was home.

Three years had passed since my last visit home, and so much had changed. Back then, I'd just started my job at the paper and was more confident than ever that I'd made the right choice when I'd left my hometown. I'd finally started to feel that the world was my oyster.

As it turned out, my oyster was full of sand and sea muck, with nary a pearl in sight.

This time, I wasn't returning home full of bravado and good news. My life was a mess, dumped upside down in a matter of weeks. And as soon as I showed up on my parents' porch, the entire town was going to know all about it.

Rosella Midnight, the odd witch out, the misfit, the weirdo.

The *cursed*.

Long-buried frustration rose, turning to a simmer in the bottom of my stomach. Swallowing, I blinked away the fuzzy blur forming in my vision, and turned the radio volume up another few clicks.

"It's only temporary," I told myself.

Karma, my small black cat, called out from her carrier on the passenger seat floorboard, giving a quiet *meow* in solidarity.

Another mile and the town came into view. Winterspell Lake wasn't a big town. There were a couple thousand people living there, making it large enough to be self-sustaining, though some residents opted to work outside the small community. The town itself was protected by magical wards, keeping it hidden from the nonmagical—those without magic. No one without magic was allowed to step foot in the town. Charms and spells concealed it, every last detail of its existence locked away. Even the highway sign I'd passed was charmed. To a nonmagical, the sign was a large, menacing no trespassing sign, with a half dozen private property signs posted beyond, in case someone didn't take the hint and kept driving.

Beyond that, sentries served as a final barrier of protection for the town. Skilled air and water mages could work in concert to form a thick fog. Earth mages could fell trees across the road, or even cause a small earthquake or fissure, blocking off access if someone were particularly persistent. And if someone managed to get past all of that, there was the bridge. It looked like the rest of the road, with dense foliage on either side, a canopy of evergreens overhead, but in reality was a drawbridge. I wasn't sure it had ever been battle tested, but it was there, nonetheless. The rest of Winterspell, including the lake itself, were fenced in with concealing charms. Animals and wildlife were free to pass as they pleased, but any human would pass through a portal spell and exit on the other side of the town, as if they'd covered a few feet, rather than a few miles.

As much as I despised my hometown, it was a rather impressive feat. Somehow made more so, after my seven years spent in the nonmagical world. The day I left Winterspell, I'd begun to suppress my own magic, but it flooded back as soon as the wheels of my car hit the drawbridge into town. A pulsating energy I couldn't quite describe. The sentries would know I was a witch and let me pass without issue, though I wasn't sure how they knew. It was one of those mysteries that teachers glossed over in school. It worked because it worked, and that was all most anyone needed to know.

"This is it," I told Karma as we drove over the bridge. The final threshold. I dialed the radio back down as I drove past the two security huts, stationed on either side of the end of the bridge. I lifted a hand to one of the guards, then told Karma, "Welcome to Winterspell."

Another soft *meow*.

The sentries didn't stop me, but as I cruised past, I caught the look on one of their faces. I was tempted to wave. "Yup, she's back. The *cursed* one. The freak. Lock up your children, or she might turn them into beasts like her."

I was exaggerating—a little. The residents of Winterspell, and the magic world at large, wouldn't run from me as though I had three horned heads, ten eyeballs, and spat green fire. But sometimes it felt like they wanted to. I saw the curious looks, the hushed whispers, the gossip.

It was the reason I'd left in the first place. In the non-magic world, I wasn't anyone special. I could blend in, live my life without worrying about what people were saying about me. Office gossip doesn't have any power after you spend the first twenty-four years of your life being a pariah in a small town.

Spelling Road, named after one of the two founding families, was the main drag through town. Shops and small businesses lined either side. Dragon's Gold Coffee Company. Merlin's Well, the town tavern. Glenda the Goode Witch's Dress Designs, named for a witch with the unfortunate name of Glenda Goode as an ode to *The Wizard of Oz*. Kaleidoscopic Potions, the town apothecary.

After a few blocks, I rolled to a four-way stop and clicked on my blinker. A right turn led me to Winters Avenue, named after the other founding family. My grandmother, Rose Winters, was the matriarch of the Winters family. She and her husband, my Grandpa Rodger, had come together with the Spelling family to build the town, nearly one hundred years ago.

Grandmother Rose was nearing her one-hundred-and-fortieth birthday, though she appeared to have stopped aging sometime in her eighties. Her mind was as sharp as ever, which she credited to the fresh air and good living, but in reality, was the result of a gift from a high fairy queen, as a sign of her gratitude when Winterspell opened its borders to a population of fairies, displaced when their patch of forest land was torn down.

According to Grandmother Rose, she had another

half a century left in her, and I believed her. My grand-father had passed away five years ago, only two years after I left Winterspell. He'd been granted the same gift of long life, but had fallen ill with a disease that even the world's best healers couldn't fix. At the time, some speculated that Grandmother might follow him quickly into the Stardust Realm, but she proved them wrong. After her time in mourning, she began anew, even starting her own business, which she ran single-handedly up until two years ago when she had an acci-dent and nearly killed herself with a deadly combina-tion of magic. That was when she'd moved in with my parents and sisters, so she could get round-the-clock care while she recovered. Somewhere along the way, her and my dad decided it would be best for him to take over the reins.

The car behind me gave a gentle honk and I snapped out of my reverie, offered an apologetic wave, and sped up. Without thinking, I'd slowed to nearly a crawl in the middle of the main road to one of the main residential areas of town. A few more houses passed, and then there it was. My childhood home. It sat up on a slight incline, which gave it a clear shot of the lake, even above the row of smaller lakeside homes, built right up along the shore's edge. My parents owned just over an acre, giving them plenty of space for the various outbuildings. My dad had a large workshop-slash-garage, set a few feet from the main house. Around back, there was a small guest cottage for my paternal grandfather, Gerald, and then a small

17

potting shed in my mother's vegetable garden. There was also a small barn, for the chickens and outdoor cats.

Exhaling, I made the final turn into the stone-laid driveway. Trees lined either side of the drive. They were bare now, dormant during the cold winter months, but in the spring they would blossom and shower the drive with tiny pink petals. The house had a farmhouse look, and was almost as old as the town itself. It was painted a navy blue, with cream trim and rustic wood beams and columns supporting the second floor. The three thousand square feet had somehow felt small when I was younger, but after years spent living in tiny apartments, it looked massive now. It struck me as funny, how my perspective had changed over time.

My dad's work truck sat at the head of the drive-way, parked in front of an open bay. When visualizing this homecoming, I hadn't been quite sure which of my family members I would encounter first. I'd hoped it would be Grandmother Rose. Of all of my family, she was the one who understood me the best. Beside my father's truck was a green station wagon. It looked relatively new, and I wasn't sure who it belonged to, although my guess would be it was my mother's. She worked part-time as a healer's assistant at the town clinic, and sometimes kept odd daytime hours.

I pulled up behind my dad's truck and parked. No sooner than I had, a tall, lanky man with salt-and-pepper hair and silver-framed glasses stepped out from the open garage. My father, James Midnight, was in his late sixties and still walked with his shoulders back and his head high. His face was long and lean, with a strong nose and angular chin. His brows were thick and often unruly, though he never seemed to notice. When I was younger, my mother used to fuss over them, smoothing them out prior to formal occasions or family pictures. Over the years, she'd given up on her quest to tame them.

Dad's hazel eyes widened behind his spectacles when he realized it was me sitting behind the wheel.

Exhaling, I cut the engine and unbuckled my seat belt. I mustered up the best smile I could manage and stepped out of the car, immediately stuffing my hands into the front pockets of my jeans. "Hi, Dad."

"Rosella? What in the—" He swung around to the house, his signature brows furrowed. "Was your mother supposed to tell me you were coming?" he asked, looking back at me.

I shook my head. "She didn't know. No one did. It was kind of a surprise. Ta-da."

He hurried toward me and we embraced, his familiar aftershave tickling my nose as my face pressed into his shoulder. "It's good to see your face."

We parted and I tucked one side of my hair behind my ear.

"How long will you be in town?" he asked.

With a soft laugh, I hitched one shoulder. "I

honestly don't know. I was kind of hoping I could stay for a few weeks, or maybe a little longer ..."

"Oh." Worry lines formed at the sides of his mouth. "Well, sure. Of course, we can make room. Um, is everything all right?"

For some reason, the question made my throat close up. I struggled against the tide of emotions, not wanting to break down into tears in my family's driveway. After a moment, I managed to pull it together long enough to offer a quick smile. "Sure. I'm just kind of in between things and need a crash pad. It's only temporary. I promise."

"Aha. I see." He removed the white shop cloth from where he'd slung it over one shoulder, and gestured up toward the house. "Your mother's in there, baking up a storm. And no, I don't know why she's doing it here instead of at the bakery." He smiled in that way long-time partners do, when they find something that still baffles them about their lover even after decades together. "Try not to give her a heart attack," he said with a wink.

I hesitated and he placed a hand on his stomach. "You know, I think I'll go in with you. I let time get away from me, and didn't stop for lunch. You hungry?"

"I could eat."

He chuckled. "Then let's get a move on."

I started to follow him toward the porch, then stopped and pivoted back to my car. "Oh, wait—" I hurried around to the passenger side and pulled out

Karma's carrier. Lowering it to the ground, I unzipped the front and released the tiny black cat. She hesitantly took a few steps out of the carrier. I smiled at her. "It's okay. You're safe here," I told her. "Just stay out of the road."

She looked up at me, her green eyes sparkling with newfound curiosity, then she jaunted off to explore the barren hydrangea bushes lining the bay of windows along the front of the house.

"I hope it's okay I brought her along," I said to my dad, replacing the carrier in the car. "She didn't have a home, and I've been feeding her for the past few months. I wasn't sure anyone would keep it up, after I left. So …" My voice trailed off as my dad started chuckling.

"Rosella, I'd almost be disappointed if you *didn't* bring home a new animal friend," he said. "You've only been doing it since you were three."

I smiled. It would be impossible to keep track of all the critters and creatures I'd adopted and cared for over the years. When I was a kid, I all but lived in the forest, playing and exploring. Any time I ran across an injured or abandoned animal in need, I hauled it home in my little red wagon, which I'd styled to look like a pet hospital ambulance.

The front door of the house burst open and a petite brunette raced out, a wide smile on her freckled face. "Ella!"

"Hi, Jazzy," I said, half a second before I was

21

engulfed in a rib-cracking embrace. I smiled and hugged her back. Jasmine and I had always been close. She was the middle of us Midnight sisters, but our youngest sister, Candice, was ten years younger than me, and eight years younger than Jasmine. A surprise baby who came into the family long after Jasmine and I had already formed a tight-knit bond.

We parted and Jasmine punched me on the arm. "Why didn't you tell me you were coming home?"

Guilt pinched at me. I'd gone back and forth on the idea dozens of times since losing my job at the paper. I should have told Jasmine. Part of me just hadn't wanted to admit it out loud. The only person I'd told was Leo, the night he came to my apartment. Before he left, I ended things, for good this time. He'd tried to change my mind, but I managed to stay strong—at least, until he'd gone and the door was closed.

"I'm sorry, Jazz. It's just been a crazy couple of weeks."

Jasmine looked at me, her hazel eyes narrowed. She could always read me.

Turning to my dad, I smiled again. "You said Mom's been baking?"

"All morning!" He lifted a brow, a slow smile spreading across his face. "Kind of gives a whole new meaning to *home sweet home*, huh?"

"Dad," Jasmine groaned, linking an arm through mine. "What are you trying to do, scare her off already?"

He chuckled and took the lead, heading up the front steps.

Jasmine held my arm a little tighter, freezing me in place a moment longer. "What's going on, Ella?"

"Later," I said, keeping my voice low. "I'll tell everyone … at dinner."

We trooped inside and scared the living pixie dust out of my mom. She dropped a spatula coated in chocolate ganache when she saw me. Samantha, the family dog, raced in to clean up the mess, getting a few good licks in before my mom shooed her off. "Rosella, what are you doing home?"

"Rosella?" another female voice said.

Grandma Rose shuffled into the kitchen. Since her accident she required the use of a cane. She'd embraced it and gotten herself some gnarled piece of wood and declared it a wizard's staff. I was honestly surprised she hadn't bedazzled it by now, with crystals and carved runes.

"Grandma!" I said, smiling as I went to give her a gentle embrace.

"What in the Nevermore are you doing here, girl?" she asked, smiling widely. "Aren't you supposed to be out there, writing exposés and taking down the mob?"

Mom sighed, rubbing her brow. "Honestly, Mother. Sometimes I wonder about you."

Grandma Rose winked at me. "Rosella knows what I'm talking about. She's destined to do big things!"

I smiled, though the pang in my heart was undeniable. Grandma Rose had always been my biggest champion, and even now, after my years spent away with a handful of phone calls to bridge the gap, she was still in my corner.

"I'm on something of a hiatus," I told her. "I was going to explain it all, at dinner, but I guess there's no time like the present. Where are Candice and Grandpa Gerald?"

"Candice is at a study group," Jasmine told me.

"And Grandpa Gerald tends to stay to himself these days," Mom said, placing a hand on Dad's shoulder.

"Come on," Dad said, going into the adjoining formal dining room. "Let's get comfortable."

Mom grabbed a tray of fresh muffins and followed.

And so, over a pile of delicious cranberry-apple muffins, I explained the situation, leaving out as many details as possible. Only Jasmine knew about Leo, and that was the way I wanted to keep it, especially now that it was over. Bringing it up now would only hurt them more. Or, at least, that's what I told myself.

"So, are you planning to go back to Portland?" Mom asked when I wrapped up.

I shrugged. "I mean, I would like to, but with the way things ended—" Despair climbed into the driver's seat of my brain and stopped all other thoughts.

"You're welcome to stay as long as you need," Dad said. "Your old room is just the way you left it, though it could probably use a good dusting."

"I'll take care of that," I said quickly.

A long moment stretched, the five of us stuck in some awkward transition where no one knew what to say or do. To be fair, the conversation had gone better than the version in my head. I'd expected more suspicion and questions. They were treating me with kid gloves for some reason, everyone doing their best to stay neutral and supportive. I appreciated it, but couldn't help wondering what they really thought of my return. However temporary it may be.

AT DINNER, I reunited with Candice and Grandpa Gerald. Candice was just the way I remembered her last time I'd visited home—bubbly and full of life, eager to jump in and tell everyone a story from her day as soon as we exchanged greetings. Grandpa Gerald, my father's father, was unfortunately not the same as when I'd left. The elderly man was withdrawn and quiet, lost inside his own mind throughout the meal. If he noticed I was there, he didn't seem interested.

After dinner, I cleared the plates and then wandered into the sunroom built off the kitchen. The room was encased with thick windows, and a brick fireplace sat at one end, allowing the space to be used in all four seasons. Grandma Rose sat in her rocking chair, watching the flames dance with a faraway look in her eyes. At my presence, she turned and smiled warmly. "You're a sight for sore eyes, my dear girl. Won't you come sit with me a moment? The fire is so lovely tonight."

I took the rocking chair beside hers, a small table separating us. Grandma Rose had a steaming mug of tea sitting there, but it didn't look as though she'd touched it yet.

"Tell me, how does it feel to be home again?" she asked.

One corner of my mouth pulled into a rueful smile. "It feels like everyone is mad at me, but they're trying really hard *not* to be."

Grandma Rose laughed softly. "Hard to pull one over on one of Portland's budding star reporters."

"Ex-reporter," I said, dropping my gaze to look at my hands.

"It's a setback, dear girl. You'll find your way."

I appreciated her confidence, even if I couldn't fully absorb it for myself.

"Are you mad at me, Grandma?"

"Mad? No, no, dear girl. I've only ever been proud of you."

My heart twisted as my eyes misted over.

"You wanted an adventure," Rose said, a gleam in her blue eyes. "I understand that better than anyone around here."

I frowned, not quite understanding her meaning. "But, you've lived in Winterspell your entire adult life."

She chuckled. "Winterspell *was* my adventure! This town was nothing but a patch of dirt when I arrived

26

here with your grandfather—may the Mother bless his spirit. Along with the Spellings, we worked to create this place from the ground up, and now I've been blessed with over a hundred years of watching it grow! I've raised my children here, and now, I've seen my grandbabies grow up and take their places." She slid a smile at me. "All except for you, my dear Rosella. You're like the puff of a dandelion, my sweet girl, born to go wherever the wind takes you."

I smiled. "I don't know how I feel about being called a weed, Grandmother."

Rose laughed; somehow the sound was still hearty even with her advanced years. The melody took me back to my childhood, stirring up the whispers of memories I'd left behind. Memories I hadn't let myself visit too often.

"Hmm." She considered the fire, then smiled. "How about this: you're a wildflower, child. Born to grow in your own way, in your own time."

"Much better," I replied with an approving nod and a little giggle.

"Good, I was running out of metaphors!" Rose laughed again. "As for the others, give them some time. Having you show up like this is quite a shock, but they'll adjust and let their guards down soon enough. They might not understand your choices, but remember, they love you no matter what you do, or where you go."

She reached over and patted my arm. "Now, dear

girl, why don't you help me out of this chair. It's been a rather exciting day, but I think I must bid it farewell and go to sleep."

I did as she asked, helping her inside, to her suite on the first floor of my parents' house. They'd renovated it to suit her needs when she'd moved in following her accident. She got situated in bed and we said good-night. I was just about to hit the light switch when she groaned.

"What is it?" I asked, turning back around.

She pushed up to sitting again, and gestured at her bedside table. "I left my darn paperback out in your dad's shop. I was out there working today and did a little reading at lunch. I must have left it behind." Muttering to herself, she threw back the coverlet and started to get up from the bed.

"Oh, Grandma, don't worry. I can go get it for you. What's it called?"

Grandmother Rose smiled. "Oh, I think you'll know which one it is. As far as I know, your father doesn't read books about bodice-ripping wizard pirates."

I blinked. "Well that certainly paints a picture."

Grandmother Rose cackled as she tucked herself back into bed. "It should be on the sill by the window. I like to look out at the water while I eat. Sometimes, I can even picture a handsome pirate coming up from the lake, soaked to the skin, in need of a hot bath, and a—"

"Grandma!"

She threw me a wink. "As they say, dear, just because there's snow on the chimney, doesn't mean there's not a fire roaring inside."

Turning, I hurried into the hall. "Here for less than a day and I already need a gallon of brain bleach. Super."

Stopping at the front door, I grabbed one of my mother's knit sweaters. I hadn't had a chance to unpack yet and didn't want to go hunting for something. After all, Grandma needed her pirate fix.

"Stars above," I said with a laugh as I slipped my arms into the sweater and pulled it around me. My mother was a couple sizes larger than me, and the sweater felt like a warm cocoon. That is, right up until I pulled open the front door and a blast of frosty air hit me in the face. I broke into a trot and hustled across the porch, down the stairs, and across the drive, to the external garage, which also housed my father's workshop.

A warm orange glow radiated from one of the garage bays and I smiled, wondering what my father was tinkering with. He was an inventor at heart, but had spent the majority of his life managing his family's business, the town bakery. He could bake a three-tiered cake without breaking a sweat, but his real passion was in enchanting work, specifically, taking normal items and making them extraordinary.

Using the side door, I let myself inside the garage. The first two bays were reserved for family storage—a collection of kayaks, paddleboards, lawn chairs, fishing equipment. Then the normal things most families kept in the garage: bulk-store packs of paper products and dry goods, storage containers filled with holiday decorations, family heirlooms and trinkets not currently on display inside the house, childhood toys and prized stuffed animals we'd never been able to part with.

The orange glow was coming from the pellet stove in the center of the third bay, the one my dad used as his workshop. The relative order of the first bay stood in polar opposition to the chaos in the workshop. My father was a brilliant wizard, but organization was not part of his skill set. Grandmother Rose had told me on more than a few occasions that on the days she worked in the shop with my father, she spent most of the time reminding him where he'd set down various tools and elements.

The shop, however, was dark but for the fire's glow. My father wasn't at his workbench, fiddling with some new invention. Instead, the light in the second bay was on, and my father's ancient truck had been pulled in, lifted up by the magically enhanced jack system he'd rigged up for working on the family cars. A pair of work boots protruded from one side, the rest of the body hidden underneath the front of the truck.

"Hey, just in here to get Grandma's pirate smut," I said, laughing to myself as I crossed through the bay toward the workshop and grabbed the paperback off the sill.

The wheels of the mechanic seat squeaked into motion as my dad rolled out from under the truck.

Only, it wasn't my dad who emerged.

A tanned face stared back at me. A handsome man, with a strong, stubble-coated jaw and a full head of tawny hair sat up on the mechanic seat. A pair of storm-cloud gray eyes peered up at me and time stopped. I'd spent hours—days—lost in those eyes, dreaming of shared wishes and hopes. There'd been a stretch of time where I'd thought I would wake up to those eyes every morning for the rest of my life.

But that had been a long time ago. Another lifetime.

"El?"

"Jake."

Jake Miller, my high school sweetheart, my first love. My first heartbreak. My most devastating goodbye.

"What—what are you doing here?" he asked, before realizing what he'd said. With a shake of his head, he tried again. "I didn't know you were back in town."

"I just got here this afternoon. It will probably take the grapevine another day or two to fully spread the word," I deadpanned. Crossing my arms, I pointed my chin at the truck. "So, you're helping my dad with this old hunk of junk? I kind of can't believe he's still holding onto it."

Jake smiled, which only made the twisted scar tissue in my heart ache even more. "Hey, don't bash it. This old girl still has a few years in her. Granted, I think at this point, it's more magic than mechanics holding her all together."

I laughed softly. "He sure does love it."

Jake reached up and rubbed the back of his neck as he used the opportunity to survey the old beast. When he looked back at me, my heart jumped. "How have you been?" I asked, trying not to stammer. "Last I heard, you were doing mechanic work full-time."

"Yeah. I, uh, took over Kenny's shop. A few years back. Kept the name, but it's mine now. I've got a couple of employees and we get enough business to keep the lights on."

A genuine smile touched the corners of my mouth. "That's great, Jake. I'm so happy for you."

"Thanks. Um, what about you? How's it going at the paper?"

My heart took a swan dive off a fifty-foot cliff. I glanced down at my slipper-clad feet. "It's *not*. I guess I'm kind of in a little bit of limbo right now, but that's all right." I met his gaze again and tried to smile. "I'll bounce back."

Jake nodded. "You always do."

There was something about the reply that stung, though I couldn't be sure if it was implied as a barb, or if my own guilty conscious was twisting it into one.

"Well, um, I guess I'd better get this back to Grandma Rose," I said, forcing a laugh as I held up the weathered paperback.

Jake offered a wry smile in return. "Aha, said pirate smut."

I cringed. After five years, *that* had to be the first thing I said to him? Mother, help me.

"Yeah. It's best if you don't think about it too much," I said, doing my best to keep from blushing as I lowered the book to my side. "It was good to see you."

The sentiment seemed to catch him off guard, but he recovered quickly. "Right, uh, yeah, you, too. I'll see you around."

"Mmhmm." I tucked my chin, then turned and high-tailed it from the garage.

As soon as I was outside, I smacked myself in the face. My cheeks were still warm. Doing my best to shake it off, I went back inside and returned the book to Grandma Rose. She thanked me, then slipped on her reading glasses and cracked open the paperback.

I started to leave, when she called after me. "Did you say hello to Jake?"

Frowning, I snapped the book out of her hands. "You *knew* he was out there?"

"Perhaps!" She babbled a laugh, a glow of mischief in her blue eyes.

"Grandma! A little warning next time." I huffed and handed the woman her book.

"He looks good, doesn't he? Aging like a fine wine."

"Goodnight, Grandmother," I said, stalking to her door, slapping the light switch on the way. "Enjoy Pirate Wesley."

CHAPTER THREE

"*I* *don't know why you didn't want to come back here. This place seems pretty great to me!*"

I smiled at Karma as she curled up on the rug in front of the fireplace. After putting Grandma Rose to bed, I'd scurried back into the sunroom and found the tiny black cat luxuriating in front of the crackling flames. "Where have you been all afternoon? I hope you didn't get into it with Flotsam and Jetsam. They were raised as house cats but decided they'd rather be barn cats and can be a little rough around the edges," I told Karma. "Personally, I blame Candice for that one. She was obsessed with dressing them up in baby clothes when they were kittens. Probably scarred the poor things for life."

Karma rolled over to warm the other side of her lithe body. Stretching her paws out overhead, she yawned, showcasing her pearly teeth. "*I don't mind being the only inside cat, although, I had to compete with that mouth-breathing dog to get any table scraps after dinner."*

I laughed. "Samantha. She's named after this TV witch, from a classic show we all used to watch."

"So, everyone here is like you?" Karma asked, peering over at me with her huge green eyes.

"Not exactly," I told her. "But yes, everyone has some form of magic. I'm the only one who can talk to animals. I'm ... special, in that regard."

Special wasn't quite the word for it. At least, not the one people in Winterspell used. To them, my ability to communicate telepathically with animals was merely a side effect of my curse, bestowed on me because of unusual circumstances surrounding my birth.

I'd buried my power, ignoring it for years, but then I'd found Karma. She'd been a stray kitten six months ago, barely weaned, and starving underneath a dumpster behind my apartment building. I wasn't technically allowed to have animals, but there weren't rules against feeding strays. So, I'd started bringing her food every day, then a couple of times a day, just to check on her. Thinking back, I still wasn't sure what made me draw up that first spark of magic. Whether it was just curiosity, or loneliness, or fate ...

The small cat was confused at first, as most animals are upon making that first contact, but we quickly bonded and when it came time for me to move out, I knew I had to bring her with me. Seeing her lounging in front of a hot fire warmed my heart in parts I hadn't even realized were frozen before.

"Well, I think I'll be very happy here, Rosella. Thank you for bringing me with you."

Smiling, I gave a short nod. "Thank you for coming with me."

We wouldn't be staying for long, but for tonight, it was nice to soak in the small comfort of a cozy fire and a contented cat.

IN CELEBRATION OF MY HOMECOMING, Mom made a full-out feast for breakfast the following morning. The entire family sat down at the long oak table in the formal dining room and dug into the mouthwatering meal.

"I even managed to get some of that seitan bacon you like at the store this morning," Mom said, placing a dish in front of me.

I'd been a vegetarian for as long as I could remember. In sharing such a unique bond with animals, it was hard to continue eating them. I still enjoyed eggs fresh from the clutch of free-range chickens we kept on the property, but kept all other animal products off my plate. My family didn't follow the same diet, but were accommodating to my desires. Mom had learned to make vegetarian dishes and the majority of the family favorites had transformed over the years.

Using my fork, I stabbed a few slices and loaded them onto my plate alongside a heaping pile of fruit salad. "Thanks, Mom. It smells great."

"There's pancakes for everyone, with fresh jam, of course," she continued, making sure everyone had a full plate before she let herself take her seat beside my father.

Everyone expressed their gratitude as they tucked into the meal. A wave of nostalgia washed over me as I looked around the table. These were the moments I'd missed. Just because it had been my choice to leave, and my history with Winterspell was complicated, didn't mean I hadn't been homesick from time to time, or that I hadn't missed my family. I had. Especially in the beginning, when I discovered firsthand just how hard it is to make it in the world on your own, especially the non-magic world.

The conversation mainly revolved around everyone's plans for the day. It was a Friday, so aside from the feast of a breakfast, everyone's days were likely set as if they were any other weekday. Mom said she had a shift at the clinic and would be leaving directly from there to attend a meeting with the local charity for which she sat on the board. Dad would be working in his shop most of the day with Grandma Rose. They'd received a large order for enchanted kitchen sponges and only had a few days left to fulfill it.

Candice would be at the library, doing her homework. She'd turned twenty that summer, but had gotten a late start to college after a year spent waffling over what she wanted to do with her life. As far as I knew, she was now enrolled in classes to help her hone her fire magic into detailed technical work that could assist her future aspirations of being a jewelry designer. Typically, young magic users graduated from high school, the same as their non-magic counterparts. But, instead of going to a traditional college, they traveled to a nearby city of their choosing where they lived in a dorm and attended classes based on their future career choice. It was a little like the college experience, but with a heavier emphasis on magic, especially if the career field required magical know-how.

After I'd graduated, I'd gone to Portland for two years, studying magical artifacts. At that point in my life, I'd thought it would be exciting to travel the world, collecting artifacts—especially the ones that could be dangerous if discovered by the non-magical. I enjoyed my time in the dorms—at first. No one else from my class in Winterspell was there, granting me a shroud of anonymity. No one knew about my secret. No one thought I was a monster. For the first time, I was just like everyone else. My snow-white hair was seen as a fashion choice, not a marking of some horrible curse.

It hadn't lasted long. By the middle of my second year, word got out. My roommate requested a room change without talking to me. Whispers and stares followed me throughout the corridors. Even my professors looked at me with a hint of apprehension.

I'd begged my parents to let me come home, but they pushed me to stick it out and complete my apprenticeship. I'd taken it as a betrayal. When I returned home, I was at the lowest point of my life up until that point. I locked myself in my room, refused to even do simple things with my family, like sharing a meal. A fog of depression settled in and no matter what anyone did, I couldn't shake it. Not my family, my friends. Not even Jake, though stars knew he tried.

Things collapsed further as time went by, relationships fraying and breaking, and eventually, my options became like tunnel vision and the only thing I could think about was getting out.

So, I did. I left. Packed up at twenty-three and went back to Portland, back to the one place I'd started to feel normal. Only this time, I didn't go to a magical school. I didn't make magical friends. I lived as a human, completely rejecting my powers and my hometown. It hadn't been easy—far from it—but the depression started to lift as I built my new life from the ground up. Every milestone I hit was of my own making, and I treasured them, clinging to them as the proof that I'd made the right decision in leaving. That was the fuel I used to get me through the homesickness or the low points where things weren't working and I felt called home.

The hardest part had come when Grandma Rose's husband, my Grandpa Rodger, passed. I stayed for two weeks, helping to prepare for the funeral, and to be there for Grandma Rose while she mourned, along with the rest of Winterspell. Toward the end of my visit, I felt suffocated by the town, but also couldn't escape the guilt over not being there when my grandfather passed, and for missing so much time while I'd been away. I'd almost considered staying permanently, and just sucking it up, but then I got the call back about the job with the paper. My dream job. My big opportunity.

I'd gone home again after Grandma Rose's accident, three years ago, and stood vigil as she recovered and then stayed to help her get settled into my parents' home. After that, things had dwindled to the occasional day trip or weekend for a birthday or holiday get-together, but I kept those trips short and often used work as an easy get-out-of-jail-free card to avoid going home altogether.

Replaying it all made me feel old. As if I'd lived two full lives already, somehow.

I stuffed the swirling emotions back down, focusing on the flavor of the food in front of me and the smell of rich coffee wafting through the dining room as Mom topped off everyone's mugs.

When she retook her seat, she cleared her throat and shot a look at my father. "So, Rosella, since you'll be here for a little while at least, your father and I thought it might be nice if you were to fill a couple shifts at the Sugar Shack, just until you line something else up. We recently had a longtime employee leave and

SPRINKLES AND SEA SERPENTS

have been running a little short-staffed while we look for a suitable replacement. I've been hoping to pick up more hours at the clinic, so it would be a real help if you could step in for me at the bakery."

"Oh." I blinked. The request didn't surprise me, but I'd figured they would give me a few days to settle in before lassoing me into picking up a shift at the family business.

The Sugar Shack was the town's bakery, and a little bit of a tourist trap. Winterspell Lake wasn't a huge tourist town, but there were a handful of two- and three-star motels in town and a campground on the other side of the lake, where magical families could come and spend the summer. My father's grandparents had started the bakery, having settled in town not too long after its founding. Sugar Shack had evolved greatly over time, from a simple, one-counter affair, into the current two-thousand-square-foot retail and production space filled with fantastical magic and confectionary wonders.

In other words, once my father got the keys to the place, it went from drab to fab. He'd pushed his parents and grandparents for years to try and spruce the place up, but they'd resisted the changes, attributing them to a young man's wide-eyed fantasy, not something practical that could improve their bottom line. At the end of the day, after full control was passed to my father, he showed them all what they'd been missing out on. My paternal grandparents gave the changes their blessing—once they saw their profits go sky-high.

"A few things have changed since your last visit," Dad interjected, a twinkle in his eyes, "but I'm sure you'll be able to pick up right where you left off."

Bobbing my head, I took another bite of maple-drenched pancake. "Sure."

"Thank you, Rosella." Mom smiled. "Jasmine, why don't you take Rosella with you when you go clock in for your shift this morning. You can get her situated."

Jasmine nodded. "Sure. We need to leave by ten," she told me.

I glanced at my watch, a no-frills piece with a rose gold face and a white faux leather band. It was already a few minutes past nine. Good thing I'd showered the night before. Still, my long tresses would need to be pulled back before I could work around food, and with nearly waist-length hair, pulling it back required a little time. Stabbing my fork at my plate, I speared fruit until I had a little kebob stacked on the tines.

Samantha came trotting into the kitchen—likely lured by the scent of the food. She was getting up there in years, and oftentimes slept through the majority of the day, but she never failed to rouse for a meal, in case she might puppy-dog-eye her way into a snack.

Dad looked down as she approached his chair. "You know what you have to do," he told her, gesturing back toward the archway into the living room.

With a doggy grin, she turned and trotted back out

of the room, only to return a minute later, her jaws gently closed around a rolled-up newspaper. My father chuckled and slipped her a slice of banana and then tore off half a pancake and passed it off to her—ignoring Mom's pointed frown.

"You spoil her," she told him.

He shrugged, smiling as the dog devoured her treat with gusto. "She's earned every bit," he said, holding up the paper.

He unrolled it, leaning back slightly as he studied the front page. His expression changed, the edges of his mouth turning down. "Well it's about time," he said.

"What is it?" Mom asked, leaning over to read the headline along with him. Her eyes widened. "Oh, dear."

"What is it?" I asked, lowering my fork.

"The warden is coming to town," Dad said, handing the paper to me.

The full headline read: *Warden Quinton Calls Emergency Council Over Missing Joggers*

"Missing joggers?" I asked, my eyes skimming the first few lines of the report.

"A young woman went missing this last summer. According to witnesses, she was spotted down by the lake early in the morning, and then was never seen again. The sheriff had a search team out looking for her day and night, but no leads ever turned up. It was as though she'd simply vanished into thin air. There weren't any signs of foul play, and no one knew what to make of it. Eventually, the search was called off and the case went cold. Then, toward the end of summer, another woman went missing. She was about the same age and description as the first, and went missing after being seen down by the lake."

I drew in a breath, bracing against the creeping feeling crawling up my spine. "What happened?"

Dad raised his brows. "No one knows. It went about the same as the first. A search party went out, searched the forest, her home, asked around town. No one knew where she was."

"My friend Beth was friends with the third missing woman," Jasmine added.

My eyes widened. "There have been *three*? In six months?"

"It's a real tragedy. Naturally, there's been a public outcry, and Sheriff Templeton called in the warden." Mom nodded, adding, "That's when they started finding their clothes."

"In the lake," Dad said, his expression solemn.

My stomach clenched. "No."

"It's all very sad," Mom said, swooping up from her seat to start gathering empty plates. I glanced at the last two bites on my plate, then decided against it and set my fork down before handing the plate to her. "I'm interested to see what else the warden's investigation has turned up."

She deposited the plates in the large, farmhouse-style sink and turned to consult the magically enhanced calendar on the side of the fridge. Little colored balls of magic dotted the boxes. She tapped one of the balls—a faded fuchsia—and the calendar shifted, the full page now displaying a detailed, hour-by-hour accounting. "I should be able to make the meeting." She swiped her fingers over the page and it returned to the monthly layout.

"I suppose we'll need to add you back on there," Dad said, turning to me as he dabbed his mouth with a sunflower yellow linen napkin. "Remind me, what color did we use for you?"

"Sapphire blue," I said, not having to think about it. The magically altered calendar was one of my father's prized inventions. He'd crafted it to easily keep track of the family's schedules. It was sort of like a magic version of a Google Calendar—without the technology limitations and glitches. Most families in Winterspell Lake had one in their homes, and they were one of his top sellers when he traveled to various magical gift shows around the country.

He snapped his fingers. "That's right. I'll have it back this afternoon."

"Thanks, Dad."

Everyone bustled from the dining room, ready for the day. I hung back a moment longer, and swiped the newspaper from the table, taking it along with me as I returned to my room to braid my hair.

My FATHER HAD WARNED me that there might be some changes to Sugar Shack, but walking through the door with Jasmine, a typhoon of memories flooded over me and it was as though no time had passed at all. Painted a soft pearlescent pink, the retail space dominated the first half of the building, a good eight hundred square feet. One wall served as a mini candy store, with a tiered display of glass containers filled with two dozen types of candies—all made in an off-site building that also belonged to my father's family. The other side of the shop was dominated by baked goods. In addition to cakes, pies, muffins, cupcakes, tarts, and cookies, the Sugar Shack also stocked everyday baked goods: several varieties of bread, dinner rolls, and even soft pretzels on occasion. The middle of the retail space was mostly left open for customers to congregate as they considered the dazzling display case, filled with tantalizing treats. Two wrought iron table and chair sets were placed in front of one of the two bay windows, the other showcasing a display of cakes and seasonal treats.

Jasmine led the way and we breezed through the retail space, heading to the back. The rest of the building was dedicated to production, with only two small rooms: one a restroom, for employees only, and another that served as the office, where the book-keeping and other managerial tasks were handled. Jasmine unlocked the door to the office and we stepped inside. The room smelled faintly of sugar and her signature peony and rose blossom perfume.

"So, you basically live here," I said, noting one of her sweaters draped over the back of one chair and a trash can full of takeout boxes as we stepped further into the room.

Jasmine sighed. "Lately, yes. Like Mom said, we're a little short-staffed at the moment. We lost a decorator in September, and then one of our bakers left last month. I have a couple interviews lined up for tomorrow afternoon. Hopefully at least one of them pans out."

"I guess it's good the place is busy at least," I offered. "Especially this time of year."

Jasmine took a seat behind the desk and rolled the chair to its edge, already reaching for the computer mouse. "Last year, a hospitality group opened a chalet-inspired resort on the other side of the lake, next to the campground. It feels like a ritzy ski lodge: huge stone fireplaces, panoramic windows in the main lodge looking out over the lake and snow-covered mountains, wood furniture and Pendleton blankets. There's no skiing around here, but they're leaning pretty heavily into the theme, with snowshoe hikes, snowmobiling, tubing. So, now, winter is just about as busy as the height of summer, tourist-wise."

"Wow. I didn't know about that."

Jasmine glanced up at me. "Well, how would you?"

"Right." I sighed and dropped into the folding chair

47

placed opposite the desk. "I'm sorry, Jazz. I know I should have called and told you I was coming back, it all just happened pretty fast."

"I noticed you aren't wearing an engagement ring. When are you planning on telling everyone else about Leo?"

My right hand swept over the left, obscuring my bare ring finger. "Leo and I broke up."

Jasmine looked up from the computer, her hazel eyes wide. "Oh. I'm sorry, Ella. I didn't realize. I thought you just weren't wearing the ring to keep people from asking about it."

I didn't bother to point out that if Leo and I were still engaged, I would have moved in with him over coming back home, even if only temporarily. There was no point in twisting that knife.

"We don't have to talk about it if you don't want to," she added.

"No," I said, shaking my head. "It's fine. I don't mind. Things were amicable. Probably a little *too* amicable," I said with a soft smile. "I think we tried to break up six times before it finally stuck. We're just in different places right now and couldn't seem to get on the same page."

Jasmine nodded, a shadow in her eyes. "I guess I know something about that," she said.

"How are you doing with all that?" I asked, holding back a cringe.

"He asked her to marry him," Jasmine said. Her

voice wasn't bitter. Just sad. "A few months ago. I ran into him at the grocery store."

I swore.

Jasmine laughed. "Yeah."

"I'm sorry, Jazz. I know that doesn't help much, but I am. You did everything you could." I wanted to reach out and take her hand, but she'd withdrawn into herself. "For what it's worth, it's his loss."

One corner of her lips curved into a half smile. "Thanks, sis."

A heavy moment of silence hung in the air for a beat before she snapped herself out of her reverie and reached for the computer mouse again. "Let me see where best to put you today. Any preference?"

"I think we both know it would be better for everyone involved if I stay away from the decorating. I can scoop cookies? I'm not bad with a spreadsheet, if there's expenses and stuff to enter." Judging by the stack of paperwork to Jasmine's left, office tasks were running a little behind schedule.

She clicked the mouse a few times, then brightened. "Got you on cookie detail from ten to four. Tomorrow is Saturday, so you remember how that goes. You'll report to Blanche. She's the baking maven around here these days."

I was bummed she didn't offer to let me stay in the office and help her with her administrative work, but I understood. "Sounds good. Anything you need before then?" I asked. "I could run out and get us some coffee, like old times."

"No need," Jasmine replied, still looking at the screen, rearranging the day's schedule. "There's an espresso machine in the break room. There are a bunch of different milks in the fridge. I think we have almond or soy, whatever you prefer."

"Oh. Wow. Sounds great. Saves me the trip across town." I rose, suddenly feeling in the way. "I guess I'll get to it, then."

Jasmine sat back in her chair. "There is one thing you should know. While we're on the subject of old flames."

Frowning, I lowered back into the chair. "Hmm?"

My sister exhaled. "I didn't want to tell you this before, but now that you're here, it's only a matter of time before someone mentions it."

My stomach lurched. "What?"

"Chloe and Jake were kind of a *thing* after you left the second time."

Shock quickly turned to anger. "Are you serious? *Chloe* Chloe?"

Jasmine nodded. "Cousin Chloe."

I swore again, shaking my head as I stared out the small window to the left of Jasmine's desk. "Unbelievable. What a snake."

"Yeah. A hundred and ten percent. She swooped in and tried to be the one to help him pick up the pieces, or whatever. At first, he put her off. He wasn't rude, but he was kind of … aloof. Then something happened, I don't know what, and things changed. They made their relationship public at the winter festival that following year."

"She always was jealous of me," I muttered. "Always sniffing around, trying to make me look bad in front of him. All through high school."

"It didn't last long," Jasmine continued, "if that helps. It was over in less than a year. I don't know the exact cause of the breakup, but knowing Chloe, she let her mask slip and Jake saw who she truly is."

"Good," I snapped. "Little harpy."

"Anyway, she manages Dragon's Gold now, so you might want to steer clear."

I barked a dry laugh. "Now I see why you had an espresso machine put in here at the bakery."

Dragon's Gold Coffee was one of two coffee shops in town, but the second, Julia's Cafe, served coffee that tasted like hot road tar. Not to mention, Julia, a fairy, would chat your ear off, making it a less than ideal spot for a quick, on-the-go cup of joe.

Jasmine smiled. "It might have weighed into my decision-making process."

"Thanks for the heads-up." I stood once again and went to the door. Pausing, I glanced back at Jasmine. "Do you want anything? Not to toot my own horn, but I did work in a coffee shop in Portland for three years while getting my degree. I make a mean cappuccino."

"I'm good. With Mom's constant refills, I probably

already had three cups with breakfast. Any more caffeine and you'll have to peel me off the ceiling."

"Sounds fun." I giggled.

Jasmine smiled. "It's good to have you back, Ella. I've missed you."

Emotion spiked in my chest. "You too, Jazz."

"Oh, and while you're down there, throw a load of towels in the wash, will you?"

Laughing, I gave her a salute and headed out.

CHAPTER FOUR

*B*lanche Mountainspring was a warm and engaging fairy-woman with a gentle but firm leadership style. I hadn't met her before, but I quickly understood why my family had put her in charge of the baking department. She was precise and organized, but managed to convey orders with a grace that kept her fluttering presence from feeling micro-manage-y.

My shift flew by as I worked down the checklist of all the items assigned to me, mainly scooping cookie dough onto trays and filling cupcake and muffin tins with various types of batter. With the sheer volume of goods that the bakery produced, the process had already started hours before Jasmine and I arrived. My job was to help the team keep things moving, so the case in front would remain well-stocked all day and was well-prepared for the weekend rush to come.

Sugar Shack played music throughout the shop, and I'd laughed to myself when it first came on. For all of my father's updates over the years, the one thing that hadn't changed was the playlist. It used to drive me halfway crazy to listen to the same songs over and over, but now, it was almost like hearing from an old friend.

Candice came to work an afternoon shift following her morning classes, and took over for one of the young women working the front counter. Candice was a people person. She loved to talk and laugh and catch up on all the goings-on with the regular customers— which were almost all of them. From my station in the back, I caught sight of her throughout the day, ringing up purchases, helping indecisive customers make their selections, and sneakily upselling just about everyone who walked through the doors. At one point, I made a comment to Blanche about how my father was going to have to find a way to keep her on the payroll once she completed her schooling, or else risk a hefty profit loss.

As for me, I liked staying in the back, out of sight. I had no doubt that word of my arrival was spreading through town. There wasn't anything I could do about that. It was part of life in a small community. Even still, it was a relief not to have to interact with any of the customers or feel their prying eyes on me while I tried to get back into the swing of things at the bakery.

Jasmine, Candice, and I took our afternoon break at the same time. We gathered around the oval table in the basement break room and dug into our respective lunches. Mom had packed a trio of sack lunches, as though we were all back in elementary school, but none of us had minded the extra bit of pampering.

"People are already talking about you," Candice told me, before biting into her sandwich.

Jasmine shot our youngest sister a warning look.

In true Candice fashion, our baby sister was decked out in a full face of makeup, her lashes long and dark, her lips painted a deep pink. Her dark brown, almost black hair was artfully arranged into a knot atop her head, with two strands pulled down to frame her heart-shaped face.

"It's fine," I told Jasmine. "It's not like I expected anything different. It's Winterspell. Where was I going to hide?"

"What I want to know is what you're doing back here," Candice said, her mouth half full. "The real story."

Jasmine muttered something and stuffed her mouth with a couple potato chips, likely to keep her from snapping at Candice. Despite living in the same small town, the two of them somehow managed to occupy completely different worlds. Candice was a classic girly-girl. If given a free afternoon, she'd spend it on YouTube, watching makeup and hair tutorials, and when she got her look down, she'd put on a bright sundress and go flouncing around town to chat with anyone and everyone. Jasmine was more like me, bookish and reserved. If she had a free day, she could be found out on the water, or at the park, under a shady tree, with a paperback and a snack.

In addition to their different personalities, it was sometimes hard not to be annoyed by the special treatment Candice received from our parents—especially our mother. She'd been born with a heart defect, and she spent the first months of her life surrounded by healers. Even after she got through the worst of it, she required special care. Jasmine and I were old enough at that point that we sometimes got left behind in the chaos of it all. It bonded us closer together, but Candice's birth shifted our family of four, setting us all on a different course.

"I told you why I'm back," I said to Candice. "I lost my job and my lease was up. I needed a place to land while I figure out my next move."

Candice studied me, her periwinkle eyes narrowed, as if she were attempting to read my mind. "So, all this time away and you don't have any friends you could stay with? Or your boyfriend?" She glanced at Jasmine. "You told me she had a boyfriend."

I exhaled. "Of course I have friends, but I don't know how long it's going to take me to line up my next move. I don't want to couch surf and live out of a duffel bag, always worried that I'm wearing out my welcome."

I left out the part about being broke. They didn't need to know that part. My final paycheck from the paper had mostly evaporated over the course of my final week in Portland. I had forty bucks to my name after filling my gas tank and paying the storage fees for a small unit to store a few of the belongings I hadn't had the heart to sell off.

Candice seemed to accept this answer, but kept a wary eye on me as she leaned back in her chair and finished her sandwich.

"I saw you take the newspaper from the table after breakfast," Jasmine told me. "Are you thinking of applying for some local jobs?"

"Oh, um, I don't think so. I guess it's just an old habit, having worked for a paper. Figured I'd catch up on local events."

"Are you going to the town meeting tomorrow?" Candice asked.

"No," I answered a little too quickly. "I'd rather jump in the lake tomorrow at dawn and catch hypothermia than go to a Winterspell town hall meeting."

"Well, that sounds stupid," she replied. "Besides, there's signs all over telling people to stay away from the water."

My brow furrowed. "What?"

"Since when?" Jasmine asked. "I just walked the trail around the lake with Beth last night after dinner."

Candice shrugged and popped the last bite of sandwich into her mouth.

Jasmine looked at me. "They've never told people to stay out of the lake before. Besides, it's the dead of winter. No one in their right mind would go into the water now."

"Not voluntarily," I said, thinking of what my parents had said about the clothing recovered from the missing joggers. "Something is definitely weird."

I started to ask Jasmine a question, when a male voice bellowed from the other side of the room, "There she is!"

The three of us whipped around. A young man with bright blue eyes and slightly overgrown sandy hair stood in the doorway, grinning from ear to ear. "There's my Candy Cane!"

"Tommy!" Candice giggled and jumped up from her chair. She all but flew across the room and launched herself into the young man's arms. They kissed passionately, making no attempt to muffle their ... uh ... enjoyment.

Jasmine huffed a sigh and sent a blast of wind surging toward the two doors leading into the break room. The wooden doors slammed shut, blocking out the couple—and their make-out noises.

"Did he just call her *Candy Cane?*" I asked with a snicker of laughter.

"He's one of her more nausea-inducing suitors," Jasmine replied dryly. "A smitten little kitten who wants to shout about his infatuation from every rooftop in Winterspell."

I giggled into my iced tea at the raw disgust in my sister's voice. Granted, she'd earned the right to sound

SPRINKLES AND SEA SERPENTS

so jaded, even though she hadn't hit thirty yet. Her last ex had sent her heart through a blender. Repeatedly. It wasn't that he was a bad guy. They just weren't right for each other. But the magnetic pull of one's first love was a hell of a drug. By the time they had finally kicked the habit for good, she was riddled with scar tissue and hesitant to ever let herself love again. Ben, her ex, on the other hand, had walked away with what appeared to be minor scrapes, and was now engaged.

Jerk.

Tilting my head, I considered my sister, wondering if I should pull at that thread. Deciding against it, I switched gears. "Well, at least she's not being snared by Grandma Rose into awkward post-romantic encounters."

Jasmine looked up from her salad. "What does that even mean? *Post-romantic* encounters?"

I told her about the little trap I'd walked into the night before, in the garage. My tactic worked, and the foggy look in her eyes vanished as she laughed at my tale of woe. "You really said *pirate smut?*"

"Yeah-huh. Sure did."

Jasmine cackled.

"I swear, that woman is always up to something," I said with a smile.

"We were all worried after her accident, but she hasn't lost a step," Jasmine agreed. "Poor Jake, though. He had to be caught off guard, too."

My smile faltered as I recalled the look on his face.

Then my mind wandered to thinking about his jaw and full lips, and the set of his shoulders …

"Uh oh," Jasmine said, yanking me from my thoughts. "I know that look."

"What look?"

"Ella, you can't," she replied, her voice gentle.

"Can't what? I'm not doing anything!" I protested.

"He's in a good place now. Don't pick at it."

Heat flashed over my skin. "I'm not going to do anything. I'd be happy if I went the rest of this visit and didn't see him again."

"Okay, good." She finished off her glass of iced tea and replaced the lid on the glass container holding the leftovers of her salad. "I need to get back upstairs. I'll see you when the shift ends."

ON MY WAY TO clock out, Blanche asked me to empty one of the trash cans before leaving. I gathered the bag, tied off the top, and carted it out the side door, to the alley where the dumpsters were stationed. With a grunt, I hauled it over the side of the nearest dumpster and brushed my hands together, though they weren't truly dirty. I took a few steps back toward the door, then stopped short. A stack of recycling was piled up in a smaller receptacle, and on top of the pile was a stack of newspapers. The *Winterspell Gazette* featured local and national news, mostly pertaining to the magic world. It came out three times a week, with the main issues delivered on Sunday morning.

The same instinct I'd had back at the house took hold and I squatted down to scoop up the abandoned papers. There were a dozen issues, a good month's worth of news. I shifted the stack under one arm and headed back inside. It was still early enough in the day that I wasn't sure what to do with myself now that my shift was over. So, I went downstairs to the break room and set the newspapers on the table. I took off my apron and chucked it into the hamper, then punched off the clock.

The smell of coffee clung to the air, as though someone had recently pulled some shots of espresso. The scent was more powerful than a siren's song, and without a lot of conscious thought, I found myself back at the machine, whipping up an afternoon cappuccino.

Once the drink was made—with perfect pillows of foam, proving I hadn't lost my touch—I settled in at the table and began perusing the newspapers, starting with the oldest issue, working forward on the timeline. Each article contained bits and pieces of the missing joggers' case as it grew. The writing provided the essential information, but seemed disjointed, leaving me to cross-check different articles to get the full story. Eventually, I got tired of flipping around and went upstairs to snag a pair of scissors from Jasmine's office. She'd gone to the bank to make a deposit, so I was able to get in and out without explaining why I needed them.

The next two hours flew by as I worked to create a timeline. Other Sugar Shack employees came and went; one or two asked what I was doing, but I didn't have a clear answer for them. What *was* I doing? I missed working at the paper, but had no interest in kicking up my journalism career in Winterspell.

I shoved aside the questions and focused on the clippings in front of me, arranging them in chronological order. As my parents had said, the first woman, Olivia Jensen, was reported missing by her friend and coworker at the Icefire Spa, part of the swanky winter-themed resort Jasmine had mentioned earlier. Olivia worked as a masseuse. She'd lived in Winterspell Lake for about a year, moving here to take the job at the spa. Her family lived in the Southwest, and hadn't heard from her in some time following her move. Her mother was quoted as saying that when Olivia called to check in, she would tell them about the chalet and her new life, but never gave many details of her personal connections. She also said she couldn't imagine why someone would want to hurt her daughter, who was a kind and generous girl with a bright future.

Olivia's rented apartment had been searched but there was no sign of foul play, nor was there an indication she'd planned on leaving town. The case went cold. Then, six weeks later, the pattern started again. This time, Amber

Fallon. She was similar in height and build to Olivia, and only a couple of years older. The story was the same. She'd last been seen by members of the Winterspell Runners, a group of joggers, mainly women, who met several times a week to do group runs on the trails around the lake. She never showed up for her work shift at the town's vet office, and her employer got worried, in light of what had happened to Olivia, and called the police.

The police investigated but turned up no leads. Amber, like Olivia, was relatively new in town and didn't yet have strong ties to the community. Her coworkers described her as friendly, but a little reserved. The police were unable to turn up any solid leads as to her whereabouts or what might have happened to her.

Another investigation. Another trail of clues gone cold. It was like the women were vanishing out of thin air.

Then the cycle happened all over again just three weeks ago. A smiling blonde woman named Krystal Conner. She was thirty-one and known to be an avid jogger. The difference was that once she was reported missing, her parents flew in from Virginia and hadn't left town since. I couldn't blame them. What was the sheriff doing? He should have every deputy and officer combing the streets day and night until the cases were solved.

Two weeks after Krystal's parents showed up, the

Warden of the Realm, Lenora Quinton, arrived and began her own investigation.

The similarities between the women gave me pause. I'd worked on a similar story during my time at the paper: a string of attacks. The missing women were all around the same age and build, though they had different hair colors and styles, judging on the photographs the families had provided for the Gazette to publish. Were they being targeted because of their looks? It seemed to be the only common thread between them—that and the running club, though I wasn't sure why that would matter, other than that maybe the attacker had spotted them during a run, and perhaps waited until they were on a solo run to swipe them off the street. If that was even what had happened. The only other thing I noticed was that given the women's birth dates, each of them would have a different elemental gift. Olivia was a water witch. Amber an earth witch. Krystal was an air witch. Could that be pure coincidence? It was a small detail but stuck in my mind anyway as I gathered the clippings together and tucked them into the outside pocket of my purse. I'd dump the leftovers back in the recycling bin on my way out. The only thing I'd accomplished was to stir up an itch that I was going to have to scratch, and unfortunately, that meant tomorrow night I'd be making my big debut at the town hall meeting.

CHAPTER FIVE

"*E*lla, you have visitors."

I glanced up from my work, scooping balls of cookie dough from a huge silver mixing bowl and dropping them onto a commercial-sized baking tray. "Me?"

Jasmine smiled. "You're the only Ella here, aren't you?" She beckoned for me. "Come on. You're going to want to say hi."

Setting the scoop and half-full bowl of dough to one side, I wiped my hands on the front of my apron and followed her to the front of the shop. The bakery was bustling, which was normal for a Saturday morning, and the voices of customers and the chime of the door blended in with the back-of-house sounds: mixers whirring, timers going off, the dozen employees working to keep the shelved stocked. For my second day on the job, Jasmine had put me with Blanche and the other bakers, and I'd been lost in thought, not paying much attention to the customers out front.

Jasmine walked me to the front of the bakery, and I took one nervous glance around at the clusters of customers milling about. To my relief, none of them looked my way. Then my eyes found two smiling faces and my heart leaped. "Sonia! Matty!" Jasmine laughed as I scrambled around the end of the display case and raced over to my two best childhood friends. Sonia Reyes, Matthew O'Lear, and me were thick as thieves all throughout school and beyond.

Sonia Reyes was a Latina beauty with tawny skin, large brown eyes, and an infectious smile. Her family was originally from Texas, but moved to Winterspell when she was just a baby, so her father could take a job teaching at our high school. Sonia was just about as tall as me, with an athletic build. She'd been captain of the rowing team our last two years of school, and from the looks of it, she'd retained her love of rowing, or moved onto some other sport that kept her in great shape.

Matty was of Irish descent with what he called "classic leprechaun" looks. Of course, none of the girls in our high school would have agreed with that assessment. He'd been homecoming king and prom king in the same year, and with his goofy, extroverted personality had also starred in the high school musical our senior year. He was a couple inches taller than me, with fair skin, thick auburn hair, and eyes the color of evergreens. The bridge of his nose and cheeks had a generous splash of freckles that darkened in the summertime. He had a squared-off jawline and was quick to smile.

We'd become friends as kids, before there was such a thing as popularity and cliques. There'd been times when I thought they might leave me behind, preferring their non-social-outcast friends over me, but it never happened. Even during the times of my depression following my apprenticeship training, they'd stuck in there with me.

Matty wrapped me in a bear hug; his stocky build felt a little softer than the last time we'd embraced, but he was still a solid wall of muscle. "I can't believe you're back!" he said, holding me at arm's length for a beat. "I've missed your face."

I laughed. "I've missed *your* face."

He passed me to Sonia and she embraced me, though it was a little tepid in comparison to Matty's, but then, not everyone could do the rib-crusher. She smiled as we stepped apart. "It's good to see you, Ella."

"You, too, Sonia. I've missed you both. You have no idea."

Sonia glanced down, tucking a strand of her long, dark hair behind her ear. "It's been a long time."

Matty slid a glance at Sonia, then took my arm and steered me to a nearby table by the front window. "Tell us everything," he said, pulling out two chairs, one for me and one for Sonia, before grabbing a third chair from the neighboring table.

We all sat down and I drew in a breath, glancing outside at the steady stream of foot traffic, trying to decide where to begin. I'd kept in semi-regular contact with them since leaving. We were linked on social media, though I didn't use it much, at least not for personal stuff. I'd certainly never shared photos of me and Leo. We had a group text conversation that we used, but those had dwindled in recent years, with months spanning between messages, to where we basically only checked in around the holidays or one of our birthdays. They'd given up on asking me to visit a couple years ago. The answer was always the same. As for them, they'd come to Portland a handful of times, spending a night or a weekend in the city. Matty had come by himself to visit me right around the time Leo and I first met. We'd stayed up all night, watching our favorite movies in my tiny apartment. I'd asked why Sonia hadn't come along, and Matty had said she was swamped with work.

Something about the look in her eyes now made me wonder if he'd been telling me the truth.

"To be honest, things didn't work out in Portland, so I'm taking a beat and figuring out my next move," I said, paring it down to the bare bone basics.

Matty gestured back toward the counter. "And you're working here again? What is this, high school all over again?"

I smiled. "Sort of feels like it, living at my parents' house, in my old room, working at the family biz."

"At least tell us we can use your discount again," Matty teased.

"I'm more interested in how you guys are doing," I said, looking at Sonia. "Are you still at Kaleidoscopic Potions?"

Sonia nodded. "Coming up on my eight-year anniversary. I'm a master-level brewer now, actually."

"Oh, wow! Congratulations. That's huge!"

"Thanks."

Matty slung an arm over Sonia's shoulders. "She's being modest. She's the youngest witch to ever get promoted to master-level in the entire Pacific Northwest! They even did a magazine feature on her in last quarter's *Potion Review*. On top of that, she coaches the high school crew team and they went all the way to nationals last year."

Sonia smiled at Matty. "Is this you trying to get me to hire you as my PR guy? Cause if so, it's kind of working."

We shared a laugh. "What about you, Matty? Besides being Sonia's hype man, obviously."

Matty shrugged. He was the kind who could find half a dozen nice things to say about someone else, but often struggled to tout his own achievements. "Same old, I guess. Still working at my dad's accounting office. Bought a new car a few months ago. She's not much to look at now, but give it some time."

Sonia smiled as she rolled her eyes. "Don't get him started talking about *Shirl*."

"Shirl?"

"Short for Shirley," Matty explained, flashing a proud papa-bear grin. "She's my baby."

Sonia pushed on his thick shoulder. "Yeah, well maybe if you spent less time in the garage, and more time at the bar, you'd meet a real-life Shirley."

"You mean like a Transformer?" Matty asked with a mischievous grin.

Sonia shoved him again, scoffing. "You are truly impossible."

I arched an eyebrow. "You can't tell me you're still single, Matty. We've gone over this before."

"He says he enjoys being single, but in reality, I think he's just spooked after that whole Armada situation," Sonia told me. "She really did a number on him. I mean, the girl's name literally means a fleet of warships; what did he expect?"

"Um, hello, I'm sitting right here," Matty protested. "And what happened with Armada has nothing to do with why I don't go out and date."

Sonia rolled her eyes as she gave me a knowing smile. "Whatever you say."

"I don't think I ever heard this particular tale of woe," I said, glancing at Matty. The last girlfriend I remembered had been two, or was it three, years ago? A snow bunny he'd met on a ski trip to Colorado. They'd gone hot and heavy for a while, but the long distance snuffed things out before they got too serious. She certainly hadn't broken his heart, and as far as I remembered, her name had started with a C ... Cecelia? Or was it Cecily?

Matty made a big show of checking his Apple Watch. "Gee, look at that, I just remembered I have to get to a meeting."

"Okay, okay," Sonia said, holding her hands up in surrender. "I'll drop it."

Matty dropped his arm down again, resting it along the back of her chair. "We're here to talk about Ella, anyway. Remember?"

Sonia nodded and clasped her hands together on the table. "True."

"All right," Matty continued, narrowing his eyes into an inquisitor's stare—which he couldn't pull off, mostly because he couldn't stop smiling long enough to manage to look intimidating. "Last time we talked, you were engaged to some hotshot photographer and talking about an editor job you were in line for. Fast-forward a few months, and now you're here ... in *Winterspell*. For good, this time. So, what happened?"

I blinked. "Who's saying it's for good? I certainly never said that. My family knows this is just temporary."

Matty hitched one shoulder. "Just town gossip, then."

Glancing around at the other customers, I wondered how many of them had already heard the same reason. Then I wondered why it even mattered. Why should I care what they think? My gaze hitched on a tall woman with a basket full of bread. She was staring at me, but quickly turned away when she realized I'd noticed, and crashed into an elderly woman who was still sporting a few curlers in her hair as she browsed the display case.

My heart sank. That was why it mattered. If it was just what people thought, that would be one thing, but it wasn't. If they could all learn to hide it a little better, maybe it wouldn't bother me.

"Leo and I ended things a few months ago," I said, a barb of pain digging into my side at the memory of our final goodbye.

"Why didn't you tell us?" Matty asked. "We could have come down and helped you drown your sorrows in a vat of that cashew ice cream you rave about."

I smiled. "Don't be too offended. I didn't talk to anyone about it. My parents don't even know I was engaged."

Sonia made a soft gasping sound. "You never told them?"

I shook my head, hot shame prickling at my skin. "He's nonmagical. A human. He's not from our world. He doesn't know anything about magic, or witches, or … any of this. They wouldn't have approved."

Matty and Sonia exchanged a quick glance.

"I know," I said a little too sharply, heading them off at the pass. "It was stupid. If I could go back in time, I would do things differently."

A lull fell over the table. Part of me wanted to bolt

back behind the counter and lose myself in the monotonous work. At least then my brain was just busy enough to keep from replaying its all-time favorite collection: Rosella's top twenty mistakes in life.

Matty cleared his throat. "I'm sorry to hear about the breakup."

"Thanks." I bobbed my chin. "As for the job, it's a long story, but I won't be going back to the paper. I've got my resume out to another batch of newspapers, so, I'm just waiting to see what happens. I don't know how long it will take, but I have no intention of staying here permanently."

Sonia's expression shifted and she gave a small nod.

"I'll keep my fingers crossed for you," Matty said, quickly drawing my attention away from Sonia. "As much as I would love to have you closer, I know this isn't where your heart is at."

A soft beep chimed and Sonia lifted her arm and hit a button on her smart watch. "Sorry," she said, leaning over to grab her handbag off the floor. "I have to get to practice." She stood and offered me a quick smile. "It was good to see you, Ella. If we don't see each other again before you leave, know that I wish you all the luck with whatever comes next."

Her cool tone took me a little off guard, but I managed to return her smile as I stood to give her one more hug. We said goodbye and she scurried out of the bakery. I watched her walk down the sidewalk and climb into a blue Subaru Forester. She pulled away from the curb and I sat back down, my heart heavy.

"She hates me, doesn't she?"

Matty sighed. "She doesn't hate you, Ella."

"Stars, I've really screwed everything up, haven't I?" I scrubbed my palms against my eyes, not even thinking about the two coats of mascara I'd applied that morning prior to arriving at work. Matty was the kind of friend who would tell me if I wound up looking like a raccoon.

"She feels like you ghosted us," Matty said, leaning back in his seat. "Which—tough love, here—you kind of did. You ghosted the whole town, El."

I couldn't argue the point. "What about you? Are you mad, too?"

He shrugged. "What would be the point? You're my friend, one of my oldest. I've been confused over the years, bummed out, but at the end of the day, you are your own person. There's no rule that says you have to stay in your hometown 'til you croak. Sonia knows that, too. I guess we'd just like to have been included a little bit more in the new life you found."

I looked down at the table, studying the swirling design in the wrought iron table painted a turquoise blue to match the bakery's accent colors.

"Don't worry about Sonia," Matty told me, seeming to read my next thought. "She'll come around. Just give her some time."

I nodded. He was probably right, but it didn't fully take away the sting. Or the guilt.

"What time does your shift end?" Matty asked after a beat. "Maybe we could grab dinner?"

"I actually think I might go to the town hall meeting tonight," I said hesitantly.

Matty feigned a heart attack, clutching his chest, rolling his eyes into the back of his head, before flopping against his chair.

I kicked him in the shin under the table. Not hard, but enough to snap him out of it. "Come on. I'm serious. Have you heard about this whole missing joggers' case?"

Matty sobered. "Of course. Everyone in town knows about it." His smile inched back across his face. "Aha. I see what's going on. Your *Harriet the Spy* side is kicking in."

He'd called me that all through school. Anytime I got an inkling about something, I was unable to resist it until the puzzle was solved. Granted, in elementary school the mysteries were pretty tame, especially in comparison to what was going on in Winterspell at present.

"You do realize you'll be walking into a fishbowl," he said.

I laughed. "Why, no. I hadn't considered that yet. You know, you're right, I should stay home and build a blanket fort and do nothing but eat pudding and watch trashy reality TV."

Matty perked. "That actually sounds pretty awesome. Count me in!"

I rolled my eyes. "I'm going to have to make my big, grand entrance eventually. At least this way I can get some information out of it."

"Plus, they serve cookies." Matty paused and considered our surroundings, then added, "Not that you're in any danger of running low."

"Ugh. Don't remind me. My mom has done nothing but stuff food down my gullet since I got here. If I don't do something quick, I'm going to have to go buy an entire new wardrobe, and considering the state of my bank account, it would be burlap chic at best."

Matty laughed. "You know, I have a gym membership, if you want to come along. I think I have an unused guest pass."

"Thanks. I might take you up on that, although tomorrow morning I might head down to the lake and take a little jog."

His grin widened. "Whatever you say, Harriet."

As it turned out, Matty and I did end up having dinner together. He showed up outside Sugar Shack when I punched out for the day, bearing two grease-splotched paper sacks. I didn't even have to see the logo to know where they were from. A huge grin broke out across my face as I hurried down the steps toward him. "Don't tell me!" I said, nabbing one of the bags. I breathed deeply. "You're an actual angel. You know that, right?"

Matty laughed and nodded his head, inviting me to follow him down the sidewalk. It wasn't three full paces before I was stuffing my face with beer-battered fries from Wimzee's, my favorite deli in Winterspell … and likely the world at large.

"Got you a falafel wrap, too," Matty said, hoisting up the second bag.

"May the Mother bless you," I said through a mouth of hot fries.

"You're acting like you haven't eaten in a month. Didn't you just tell me that Penelope has been feeding you round the clock since you showed up?"

Laughing, I nodded and swallowed the bite. "She has. But, I was kind of on a ramen and scrambled egg diet for the last two or three weeks, so I'm giving myself another week to make up for lost calories."

"Aha." He took a foil-wrapped cylinder out of the bag and passed it to me, trading for the bag of fries. "Well, then you need some protein. Here. There's extra dressing in the bag, if you want it."

Gratefully, I accepted the falafel wrap and tore into the foil, only slowing a little.

"You still set on going to the town hall meeting?" he asked, though I noted we were already walking in the right direction.

"I think so." I took a bite and groaned. "Ugh. It's even better than I remembered."

Matty laughed and nibbled a few fries as we continued on our way.

"I figure we can get there a few minutes late, when most everyone will already be sitting down. That way, we can slip in the back, and no one will even notice."

"You've got this all planned out, huh?" Matty grinned. "Just remember, if we're too late, and Wilson has already launched his opening monologue, he'll stop the whole thing just to give us that sour, lecturing look he used to give us in high school."

I groaned, the expression permanently etched into my memory. "Right. I forgot that he'd taken over the town council."

"Gleefully," Matty said, rolling his eyes.

Wilson Peabody was the high school principal and now head of the town council. He was a stickler for rules—big and small. A pedantic man with no life outside of his work. Likely because no one would put up with him long enough to form a lasting relationship. I couldn't imagine being romantically involved with someone like that. He probably made the bed each morning with hospital corners, would flip his lid over the toaster settings getting budged, let alone the TV volume or thermostat temperature. He also probably had a sock drawer that would make Mister Rogers look like a slob.

"And as soon as the warden is done speaking, we

slip out again," I told Matty. "I have no interest in standing around small-talking."

Matty smiled. "As long as you promise to slow down long enough for me to grab a fistful of cookies on the way out."

Laughing, we walked a little further and the town hall came into view.

The Winterspell town hall was one of my favorite buildings. It was white, with a spire and huge wooden doors painted a navy blue so dark they almost looked black. As we were nearing the holiday season, the lights were already strung, and two giant wreaths hung on the doors with bright red bows. In spring, the trees lining the wide walkway would be lush and green, but they'd dropped their leaves and were now wintery branches draped in soft, twinkling lights. Two potted holly bushes flanked the doors, and those too were decorated with twinkling lights. Next month, in December, they would be decorated with gold and silver ornaments, long tapered baubles that looked like glittering icicles.

The doors were closed against the chilly weather, and none of the attendees lingered out on the steps or walkway like they would if the weather were warmer, catching up with friends and chit-chatting about the day's events before going inside to find a seat. Tonight's event would be packed, and no one was wasting any time lingering outside.

I stopped short of the stone steps, the fries and

falafel sitting a little heavy in my stomach. Matty took the first two steps, then turned back, realizing he'd lost me. He smiled at me. "Come on, El. You're going to have to show your face eventually. Think of it like ripping off a Band-Aid."

I winced. "A Band-Aid I've been wearing for the better part of a decade?"

"Come on," Matty said, taking my elbow to steer me forward.

Exhaling, I let him propel me up the front steps, onto the wide porch that wrapped around one side of the building, where two sets of French doors could be opened for large events.

At the top, Matty reached for the door. Pulling it open, he offered me an encouraging smile. "Lights, camera, action."

CHAPTER SIX

*G*iven the feature in the town newspaper, the open meeting area was packed, with standing room only along the outside edges of the mostly seated crowd. Normally, the town meetings drew a much smaller segment of Winterspell's population, the die-hards who needed to be involved in every aspect of town life, and those who were there only to present their requests or complaints (usually complaints). Tonight, the large town hall, an original building to Winterspell, held a good three hundred people, all crammed together in an assortment of pew benches that looked borrowed from the neighboring church, folding chairs, a few rolling chairs, and it looked as though some residents had toted along their own lawn chairs in anticipation of the swarm.

So, not only was I making my debut, but I was

doing it in front of a much larger audience than I'd anticipated.

Just swell.

Matty kept a hand on the middle of my back as we moved through the throng, jockeying for places in the back of the room. It was a small gesture, but went a long way in keeping me calm—and from bolting from the building like my hair was on fire.

As expected, I left a ripple of double-takes and whispers in my wake as we moved through the crowd. When we finally managed to find a place to stand, in the left corner of the back wall, people were openly staring.

Matty kept his hand firmly in place and I scooted a little closer into his side. "Ignore them," he murmured close to my ear.

At the front of the room, Walter Peabody took the stage. He hadn't changed since my high school days, other than maybe adding a few extra pounds and more gray hair. He wore a pair of round spectacles that made his beady eyes look huge and almost bug-like. A perfectly trimmed mustache brushed up against his thin lips. As predicted, he wore an argyle sweater vest over a starched white shirt. I would have bet anything that the jacket he'd worn earlier in the day had patches on the elbows and a pocket protector.

"Good evening, ladies and gentlemen," Walter said, his voice amplified by a small microphone. His magnified eyes roved the room, stopping abruptly when they landed on me and Matty in the corner.

"There's that *no talking in detention* look we've missed so much," Matty whispered with a laugh.

I smiled and started to relax a little bit.

Walter forced his gaze away from me, and continued. "As you all likely know by now, our Warden of the Realm, Leona Quinton, has traveled to town to speak tonight, concerning the missing women. As such, we will hold off all normal council business until next week's assembly." Walter reached up and fidgeted with the knot of his tie. "Now, if you'll please join me in welcoming Warden Quinton to the podium." He took a couple steps back, offering a polite applause as a tall woman with broad shoulders and warm brown skin took over the microphone. She wore long gray robes and her black hair was pulled back in a tight bun, almost like a female soldier would wear under her service cap. She was lean and strong, with sharp eyes and a full mouth that formed a straight line over a pointed chin.

I wasn't sure how old Leona Quinton was, but if I'd had to guess, I'd have placed her in her mid-forties. To become the Warden of the Realm, one had to serve as an Agent of the Arcane Order, and it would have taken decades of work to prove oneself fit for such a huge responsibility. Leona had likely started her career path right out of high school, choosing the appropriate apprenticeships for her post-studies.

"Thank you, Mr. Peabody," Leona said as the round of applause faded. "As most of you know, my office was called in to join Sheriff Templeton's investigation into these tragic disappearances."

Leona glanced at someone in the front row, and I recognized the sheriff's hat. I couldn't see his face from my vantage point, and I wondered how he was handling having the warden come in and effectively take over his office's investigation. Sheriff Templeton was a legacy selection, having taken over the position for his father fifteen or so years ago. Winterspell chose their sheriff via an election every four years, with every resident able to cast a vote, but Winterspell was resistant to change, and I often thought most people simply circled the Templeton name on the ballot without giving it much thought beyond that. After all, a Templeton had held the position for some sixty years now; why change it up?

Still, this case with the missing women was the highest-profile case I could recall in all my time in Winterspell. And from my brief but deep dive into the case, it didn't seem as though Templeton was providing much by way of results. It made me wonder if maybe the residents of Winterspell would study their ballots a little closer come the next election. He had to be in crisis mode, if not for the sake of the missing women, then at least for his own career.

From the podium, Leona continued, "Along with a team of Agents of the Arcane Order, I have concluded

my investigation into these sad and tragic disappearances."

Everyone in the room took a collective breath. I
glanced up at Matty. He looked just as taken aback as I
felt. The case had been solved?

Leona took an agonizing pause, her gaze momentarily stuck on a couple in the front row, on the other
side of the aisle from the sheriff. After a moment, she
squared her shoulders and continued. "There is a sea
serpent in the lake. At present, I do not know where it
came from or how it made its way into Winterspell
Lake, but I have determined that it is responsible for
ending the lives of Olivia Jensen, Amber Fallon, and
Krystal Conner." She glanced at the couple again, her
eyes sorrowful.

A burst of whispers broke out, as townsfolk turned
to one another with expressions of shock, outrage, and
panicked questions. Leona let this continue for a
minute before she asked for order and silence.

"I understand this is quite a shock," she said.
"Nothing like this has happened here before, but it's
not entirely unprecedented. While sea serpents are
rare, there have been strings of attacks like this
reported in other places. I'm afraid that evidence here
shows the same pattern."

The whispers kicked up again. Leona changed
tactics. She made a beckoning motion at a dark-haired
man standing near the front of the room, his broad
shoulders against the wall. At her command, he

marched up to the podium, giving a respectful nod as he took his place at her side.

"Who is that?" I whispered to Matty.

He shrugged, his expression baffled. "I have no idea."

The man was taller than the warden, which was saying something, as Leona looked to be nearly six feet tall, an almost Amazonian woman. He had shoulder-length jet-black hair, with tanned skin, dark eyes, and more than a few days' worth of stubble on his sculpted jawline. He wore black pants and a cobalt blue sweater. Even "at ease" he looked ready to spring into attack mode at the drop of a dime. There was something restless and intense about his posture and the look in his eyes.

"This is Orion Croft," Leona said, gesturing at the man. "He works for the Order, serving in a specialized department that handles the tracking and elimination of dangerous creatures."

I blinked. "So, wait, he's a *monster hunter*."

Matty snorted. "Can I just say, I'm glad you dragged me to this meeting. This is far better than anything I was going to watch on TV tonight."

I started to smile, then needled him with my elbow. "Shh."

Admittedly, things were more interesting than I'd expected, but there were still three dead women to consider, which made it hard to be entertained by the sheer spectacle of the whole thing.

"Orion will be tracking and eliminating the serpent before further harm can come to anyone in this community," Leona announced. "In the meantime, signs have been posted along the shore of the lake, warning residents and visitors to steer clear. Unfortunately, I have Order business to attend to, and will not be able to stay in town beyond tomorrow morning. However, I have complete confidence in Mr. Croft. My condolences are with those who have lost a daughter, a friend. There will be a vigil for the three victims next weekend, to give everyone a chance to gather and mourn together."

With a gracious nod, Leona stepped aside, handing control of the meeting back to Walter. For a moment, I was surprised she hadn't opened up the floor to questions, but then, looking around the room, I couldn't blame her. The crowd wore a mixture of expressions; some looked satisfied, others were softly crying, leaning into one another, while others looked baffled and confused, then there were a sprinkling of those whose expressions radiated shock or varying shades of anger.

As for myself, I wasn't sure what I felt. The explanation the warden presented made sense logically, but there was something gnawing in my gut. Maybe it was my Harriet senses, maybe it was my journalistic training, maybe it was good old-fashioned intuition, but something was tingling, pressing for more answers.

Answers I didn't have.

At least, not yet.

Another part of me was sad for the serpent. I would never voice that part to anyone else—the town already thought I was halfway to being a monster myself. But the serpent wasn't likely to be some cold-blooded killer, attacking for fun or the thrill of the kill. The serpent was probably hungry, or trying to defend themselves, or … Mother forbid, their offspring. Which opened another question. How on earth had the creature even gotten into Winterspell Lake? There weren't any channels flowing to or from the body of water. Meaning … someone dumped it there?

I supposed it wasn't out of the realm of possibility. Perhaps the poor thing had started out as someone's ill-advised house pet, and when it grew too large, was released into the lake. Sort of a Manhattan-sewer-alligator situation. Only on a much bigger—and far more deadly—scale.

At the podium, Walter was addressing the crowd with details of the vigil Leona had mentioned. After that, he dismissed the meeting with a bang of his (very official and not at all silly) gavel.

Matty exhaled. "Well, that sure was something, huh?"

I started to reply, when a red-haired woman with a baby strapped to her chest stormed up to me, one finger waggling. "This is all your fault! You probably released that beast into the lake and now it's doing your bidding!"

"Whoa!" Matty boomed, inserting himself between me and the woman. "Back off, lady! You have no idea what you're talking about."

The woman glared at me and Matty shifted, concealing me entirely behind his thick torso. "Move along," he barked.

Reluctantly, the woman moved along with the crowd—most of whom were staring at me even as they shuffled toward the exit. A fresh batch of whispers stirred as the huffy woman barged her way out the doors.

"Sweet Mother," Matty muttered, turning back to face me. "Are you okay?"

I nodded, barely holding back the tears that rushed up as soon as Matty had stepped between me and the crazed woman. Sighing, Matty placed his hands on my arms, anchoring them firmly as though he thought I might try to bolt. "She's some ignorant whack-a-doo, El. You can't let her get inside your head. Any rational person knows that you had nothing to do with this whole mess. I mean … the nerve. Ugh."

Tucking me under one arm, he nudged his chin toward the other end of the hall. "Come on, let's go out the back."

"I saw you and Matty at the council meeting."

Jasmine settled down in the chair beside me, her

89

hands wrapped around a cup of hot tea. She'd offered to make me one when she'd first entered the kitchen, but I'd turned her down. In front of me my laptop screen blared a coral-pink glow.

"I think the entire town saw me at the council meeting," I mumbled, still shaken from the nasty encounter at the tail end. Matty had walked me home after I opted out of going to get a drink with him at the local watering hole. He understood, and we'd made plans to see each other the following afternoon. After changing into pajamas, I'd taken my laptop to the dining room and started working on my computer, with Karma curled up in my lap.

Jasmine smiled softly. "Yeah. I saw that part, too. Matty looked like he had it in hand, so I stayed out of the way. But, you know I would have blasted her right out into the street by the trash cans, where she belongs, if he hadn't."

A ghost of a smile lifted my lips. "I do. Thanks."

Jasmine could have done it, too. She was an air witch with more power than most. When we were younger, she crafted herself a pair of wings and used to fly—well, it was more like hang gliding, but she called it flying—around town. Naturally, every other kid in town wanted a turn and for a little while she was charging kids five bucks a trip around the high school football field. She'd amassed a tidy little sum of money before the other kids' parents stormed our parents' front yard, demanding that the so-called "flying lessons" stop before someone got seriously injured.

"I'm sorry that people are so cruel," Jasmine said, her smile fading. "I think it comes from a fear of the unknown, but that's a sorry excuse for it."

Karma twitched in her sleep and I smiled down at the way her whiskers bounced and quivered. I wondered what she was dreaming about. I'd have to ask her when she stirred.

"I'd rather just forget about it, I think."

"Whatcha working on?" Jasmine asked, leaning over to see my computer screen. Squinting, she read the top line. "A travel blog? This is yours?"

"Yeah. It's kind of what I work on when I need a distraction."

She sat back in her seat and sipped at her steaming tea. "I didn't know you had a blog."

"Well," I cringed, "it's unpublished. More of a pipe dream than an actual *thing*, at this point."

"The layout looks pretty good. Why not publish it? Isn't that kind of the whole point of a blog? To have people read it."

I smiled. "I know. I know."

"What's holding you back?"

I shifted a glance at my sister. She knew me too well. "I haven't gone anywhere all that exciting. At least, not yet. I thought that—" I stopped short, an old pain lashing out unexpectedly. My lips twisted to one side

91

as I struggled to contain my emotions. "It was something I was going to do ... with Leo."

Jasmine's dark brows lifted in understanding. "Oh."

Closing the laptop, I sighed. "Old dreams die hard, right?"

Jasmine set her mug on the table. "You don't need Leo to travel, Ella. That's what you're doing here, right? Getting your feet back under you so you can go off on the next adventure. So, you work at the bakery for a few months, or however long it takes, while you plan your trip."

"Thanks, Jazz."

"For what?" she asked.

"For always believing in me. I know it hurt you when I left, but you were one of the only ones who never asked me to reconsider. It's like you've always known I wasn't meant to stay here."

She tucked her chin, lowering her eyes for a moment. When she lifted them back to mine, a gleam showed at the corners. "It's been hard, El. Not having you around. Especially with—" Her words choked off and a single tear slipped free. Reaching over the table, she took my hand and squeezed. "I'll be okay if you leave again, but you have to promise it won't be like last time. I don't want to lose you again."

Emotion swelled in my throat, leaving me momentarily speechless, so I nodded and squeezed her hand back. "I promise."

CHAPTER SEVEN

*N*O SWIMMING ALLOWED. STAY OFF THE SHORE.

Frowning at the sign, I jogged past it. I'd snagged a wet suit from the garage—one of the many summertime toys my family had acquired over the years. It wasn't made for deep sea diving or anything, but it would help keep me from going hypothermic long enough to do what I needed to do.

I paused on the shore, studying the still-dark outline of the towering evergreens and the way the mountain peaks reflected off the lake's smooth-as-glass surface. It was early. I'd sneaked out of my parents' house just before five a.m., grabbed the wet suit, and jogged down to the lake. There were public restrooms in the parking lot of the rest area, right along the water's edge. They'd been left unlocked, so I slipped into one of the stalls and changed out of my leggings and oversized T-shirt and put on the wet suit.

It was still quiet as midnight, but I had to hurry. The town early birds wouldn't sleep forever. I stashed my clothes on a park bench to retrieve later, and then pulled my hair back into a quick and messy braid. Just in case, I went about a mile down the shore. I hadn't wanted to risk the engine noise of my car waking my family, so I hoofed it through the sand, frequently checking over my shoulder to make sure no one had followed me.

A ridge rose from the shore, covered in stubby shrubs and tree sprouts never destined to grow tall. It stretched out into the water, essentially ending the smooth shoreline where families liked to gather and play when the weather was warm. Climbing the ridge wasn't fun, with the rocky terrain making it hard to find purchase, but it dropped down onto a secluded patch of sand. It was a well-known high school make-out beach, or where kids went to party and drink after dark. Cigarette butts and a few broken beer bottles littered the sand and I was glad I'd kept my shoes on.

Scoffing, I picked carefully past the mess. "This is why we can't have nice things."

Ash and charred driftwood sat in a circle, marking the location of the last bonfire. I stopped at the water's edge and took off my sneakers. Exhaling, I stood and braced myself for the plunge. It was going to hurt, there was no way around that. The secret was to not panic.

My eyes fluttered shut as I sent out a tendril of magic. It skimmed the surface of the lake, then plunged below. The last thing I wanted to do was dive in and immediately have my face eaten off by a sea serpent. My magic brushed against my mind, alerting me to small creatures close to the shoreline. Nothing bigger than a trout.

Recalling the magic, I drew in a steadying breath and tensed my muscles. "It's now or never."

Squeezing my eyes closed, I raced forward and dove into the ice-cold water. They popped open, wide with the shock as I submerged myself. My face burned with the cold, stinging and searing. My pulse spiked as fight-or-flight kicked in and I took a beat to battle my instincts to run away.

I'd come here for a reason. I had a purpose.

Forcing my thoughts to calm, I let the darkness wash over me as I swam out further from the shore, pumping my legs underwater as much as possible to keep from splashing about. With my mind centered, a channel opened and I was once again able to send my magic out ahead of me. Searching.

Where are you?

The sensation was strange. It had been so long since I'd opened my magic up in this way. Little quips with Karma were nothing compared to the effort it took to send my magic out on a hunt. With Karma, there was a clear target for the magic to work, but this …

This was entirely different. It was a long shot. But I had to try anyway.

My body temperature continued to drop. The wet suit could only do so much. My face, calves, and feet were exposed. The suit was meant for the chilly but much warmer summer temperatures, when the water still had a bite. This wasn't a bite. This was a great white shark trying to devour me whole.

Stop it, Rosella. I forced my mind calm again, and sent out another wave of magic, throwing more power behind it.

I waited. My heart sinking.

My plan had failed.

Wait!

My eyes flew open. I couldn't see the creature lurking in the dark waters ahead, but I knew it was there. They'd heard my magic calling and came closer to investigate. My heart popped up like a champagne cork and slammed against my ribs. Diving into a lake on a sea serpent tracking mission was likely in the top five craziest things I'd ever done in my life. Especially when all I knew about the creature was that it was facing the blame for a series of deaths—of young women, all who had a heck of a lot in common with me.

I'm not going to hurt you, I told the large hulking presence.

The words flowed into the water, silent messages carried along by pulses of still more magic.

"Who are you?" The creature's reply sounded in my mind, as clearly as if someone standing beside me had said it.

My lungs burned. I couldn't hold my breath much longer, not while fighting the chill. *I promise I will explain. Come to the shore. I'm not here to hurt you.*

I surfaced, gasping for air, then quickly swam away —trying to ignore the fact that I was exposing my backside to a potentially deadly creature.

Right. Again, not my most brilliant plan.

Hustling along, I climbed out of the sand and jogged back a few steps. Along with the wet suit, I'd also swiped a few chemical heat packs and a lighter from the kit in the garage. Tucked inside my wet suit, they'd been kept safe from the water. I fished them out and crushed the first heat pack. The chemicals inside mingled and within seconds I had a hot pad to warm my fingertips. I held it in my hands, waiting for the feeling to return to my frozen fingers, then set about making a small fire while my teeth chattered.

As I worked, I kept an eye on the surface of the lake, which had gone smooth once more. The small fire was just starting to sputter to life, burning through the small twigs, when the water moved. My breath hitched in the back of my throat as a sleek, mauve head rose from the ripples. Fins fanned away from the creature's head, pointed bony spindles covered with a webbed skin. Bright emerald green eyes stared at me, wide and wild.

From where I stood, I couldn't tell how big the serpent was, but judging by the long, swan-like neck, there was quite a large body underneath the water's surface.

Let's just hope this one can't breathe fire, I thought to myself as I stared, awestruck.

The serpent lifted its head and I noticed the multi-colored scales ran down the length of its neck. *"Who are you?"* the creature asked.

"My name is Rosella Midnight. I'm a witch." I squared my shoulders. "I came to ask you a question."

The serpent canted its head. *"A question?"*

"Over the course of the past several months, three women have gone missing—stars, for all I know, the count is higher. The people in this town think you are responsible."

The serpent reared back, seemingly startled by the accusation. I braced as anger flared in the emerald eyes, setting them ablaze.

Holding up my hands, I spoke quickly. "I'm—I'm not saying you did. I'm only here to find out the truth."

"I don't eat flesh," the serpent hissed in reply. *"At least, not human flesh. I am a strict pescatarian."*

"Really?" I blinked. "I'm a vegetarian, so I get that."

As soon as the words left my mouth, I did a mental face-palm.

Great, Rosella. Become best friends with a sea serpent.

That should make for an interesting slumber party. In fact, why don't you lasso it with a leash and take it for walks around town. Everyone thinks you're a freak already, why not run with it?

"You're very odd," the serpent told me.

I barked a laugh. "You have no idea."

Lowering slightly, bringing its powerful jaws level with the water's surface, the serpent considered me for a long moment. The emerald eyes changed, becoming almost catlike in their intensity. Karma often shared that expression when watching a lazy housefly, wondering if chasing it would be worth the effort.

"Do you have a name?"

"*I was once called Valkyrie,*" the serpent replied, "*but the one who gave me that name is no longer with me, so now, I choose to be free of cages and chains and names.*"

"Chains? Who would want to chain you?"

Not to mention, how would that even work? Did she have limbs underneath the surface? It seemed like that would kind of work against the whole *serpent* part of her species, but what did I know?

"*It is a long story, and I do not wish to tell it.*"

"Fair enough." I nodded. "Listen, I need you to know that there is a man who has been tasked with hunting and killing you. As I said, the people in town think you're responsible for killing three women, and they won't rest until you're ... eliminated. I don't know if it's possible, but if you can find a place to hide, you should. I'll do what I can to try and stop him."

"I cannot leave this lake. It is my home now."

"I understand, but just … try to lie low for a few days. I'll work as fast as I can, but you can buy me more time by making yourself hard to find. Do you have any magic that can help? Like a cloaking mechanism or something?"

The serpent shook her head. *"No. I was bred for battle. When it became clear I was not a good monster of war, I was dropped here."*

War? Bred? A half-dozen questions popped into my mind, but I shoved them down. There wasn't time for that now. The only thing that mattered was keeping her safe until I could convince the warden to reconsider the death sentence she'd handed down.

"Stay hidden," I told her once more. "I'll come to you, just like today, as soon as it's safe."

The serpent nodded and without another word, slipped back beneath the lake's surface, vanishing.

The eerie predawn silence washed over me and I hoped I hadn't just made a promise I couldn't keep.

I LEFT the lake and made my way back to my parents' house, stopping only to change back into my leggings and sweater. Things were still quiet when I stashed the wet suit back in the garage and tiptoed to the hallway bathroom to take the hottest shower of my life. It was Sunday morning. That usually meant a slow start, a big breakfast, and lots and lots of coffee. Knowing I was too wired to ever get back to sleep, I started a fire in the living room and then wandered back into the kitchen and got a jump on the caffeine.

Karma joined me in the kitchen, brushing her silky smooth face against my ankles while I waited impatiently by the coffee pot, mug in hand. As soon as there was enough to pour, I filled my cup and then replaced the carafe to finish the brew. As I sipped the first mouthful of hot coffee, I sighed happily. My hair was still wet—as I hadn't wanted to wake everyone with the blow dryer—but it was tucked up into a towel, away from my shoulders. The coffee warmed the parts the steam-filled shower hadn't, and I settled down in front of the crackling fireplace, Karma on my lap.

"Told you it was better to be a house cat," I said, smiling down at the purring ball of fur.

It didn't take long for my thoughts to wander back to the fantastical encounter with the sea serpent. Part of me wondered if it hadn't all been some kind of crazy dream. But the memory of the biting cold quickly dispelled that theory. Even in magic-fueled dreams, nerves and reflexes didn't work like they did when conscious. No, I'd been reckless enough to dive into a near-frozen lake to try and talk reason into a woman-eating sea serpent.

Although, now I knew better. Valkyrie hadn't killed those women. Which left one question. One that was colder than the lake itself.

Who had?

A shudder ran up my spine. I didn't have the answer, but I wouldn't rest until I did.

The Midnight household slowly came to life over the next two hours. Mom came downstairs first, and I nearly gave her a heart attack. She'd yelped upon coming in the kitchen and seeing my silhouette against the flames in the fireplace. As soon as she recovered from the surprise, she set about making another big breakfast. I moved Karma out of my lap, against her protests, and went to help.

Mom was in her sixties, but she didn't look it. Her body was soft and round, from good food and a comfortable life. Her hair was like my two sisters', dark enough to be mistaken for black in certain lighting. She was wearing it shorter than I remembered it ever being before, but it still reached the tops of her shoulders. A fire witch with a warm, caregiver personality, who always looked after others first.

"How's it been at Sugar Shack?" she asked, handing me a basket of eggs that had been collected from the backyard chickens. "I'll bet it's weird to see it so busy when it's not a holiday weekend."

I laughed softly and began cracking eggs into a big ceramic bowl. "Definitely, but I'm happy for you guys. Dad's worked really hard to get the place to this point."

She nodded, a wistful look in her sparkling blue eyes. "Indeed, he has. I'm just grateful he's now able to use his talents in a more direct manner. He was starting to drive everyone crazy, being down at the bakery all the time. You know how he gets when he's bored."

My lips quirked. "Fixing things until they break?"

Laughing, she pointed at her nose. "That's it."

We shared a laugh as we cooked. Soon enough, Jasmine, Grandma Rose, Grandpa Gerald, and my dad all joined us. Candice was the last to arrive, having taken the time to primp and prep before family break-fast. She flounced into the room, all bright-eyed and made-up like she was making a pit stop on her way to a photo shoot for a cosmetics company.

Samantha brought the paper in and my father rewarded her with a slice of bacon. She carried it happily into the living room, tail wagging. The front page was dominated by an article detailing the events of the town hall meeting. I didn't bother asking if the reporting included a blow-by-blow account of the unhinged woman accosting me on her way out the door.

"Looks like they've set up a tip line," my father said, gesturing halfway down the page. "That Orion fellow will be working with the sheriff's department to track and kill the beast."

"Oh, yes," my mother sighed. "Templeton was out in the parking lot, holding court, telling anyone who would listen all about how he planned to skin the thing in the town square."

Candice made a gagging noise and gingerly set her fork down.

"Hmm. Well, he's going to have to make up a lot of ground if he's going to hold off a challenger next year. The town isn't likely to forget this anytime soon," my father replied, refolding the paper.

The conversation shifted away from the investigation into the sea serpent as my mother asked what everyone's plans were for the day ahead. Sugar Shack's production was closed on Sundays, with only a few front house staff working to sell off the day-old breads, pastries, and cakes. My father and grandmother would be back in the workshop—they didn't believe in days off. My mother was running errands, and asked us all to write down things we needed from the store on her notepad by the microwave before taking off. Candice was going out with friends—hence the look. One must be Instagram-worthy at all times when in a social setting. Jasmine was cagier with her reply, but told me privately, while we cleared our plates, that she'd be back for lunch in case I wanted company.

"Oh, I think Matty and I might go hang out," I told her. "I'll text if my plans change though."

Jasmine smiled and waved me off. "Don't worry about it. I'm glad you two are catching up. What about Sonia?"

I frowned. "I think she might need a little more time to warm up to me being back."

Jasmine gave an understanding nod and didn't press the issue. "What are you doing this morning?"

I twisted the end of my braid, the strands still slightly damp from my little predawn dip in the lake. I hadn't told anyone about meeting Valkyrie, and I wasn't going to either. But I also didn't want to lie to Jasmine—to any of them. "I was thinking I might go for a drive."

Which was true. I planned on driving to wherever this supposed monster hunter was and pleading with him to hold off on the hunt.

"It must be a big shift, being back here," Jasmine said, glancing at the table where Mom and Grandma Rose sat, chatting as they drank their last cups of coffee. Grandpa Gerald had shuffled back to his cottage as soon as the meal was over, barely giving more than a few grunts in reply to questions when Mom tried to engage with him.

"I remember feeling sort of … suffocated, after I moved back home," Jasmine continued. "It takes time to adjust from living alone to being under the same roof with six other people."

Smiling, I nudged my chin toward Samantha who had come back into the dining room to beg for leftovers. "Not to mention the menagerie."

Jasmine sighed. "Yes, them, too."

"Thanks for the invitation, Jazz. I'll call you when I'm free."

We said goodbye and I went down the hall to my

bedroom to slap on a little makeup. I didn't have Candice's skill level when it came to cosmetics, but I usually wore a couple coats of mascara when going out and about. Thanks to my ... gift ... my lashes were devoid of all pigment, leaving them the same snow white as the rest of my hair. My skin was also fair and lacked color without a little help. I swirled on a layer of mineral makeup, giving me a boost of sunscreen in the process, because even in the dead of winter, my skin was apt to burn, especially with the sun bouncing off the lake's surface. A swirl of blush and a swipe of berry lip gloss, and I was done. The entire process took less than three minutes. Candice would be no doubt horrified.

Grabbing my purse, a beaded satchel that hung across my body so I didn't have to fuss with it, I headed out. I drove to Dragon's Gold Coffee, purchased my own copy of today's newspaper and a green tea, and went back to my car. Safely behind the wheel, I found the sheriff's tip line and dialed. Someone answered on the first ring, a female with a high-pitched, nasally voice. "Sheriff Templeton's sea serpent hotline."

I rolled my eyes. Of course he'd branded it.

"Yes, hello, I have information to share with the Order's representative," I said, tapping my fingers along the top of the steering wheel.

"Excellent! Let me just grab my pen." A soft rustling sound. "Okay. Go ahead."

"I think it would be better in person. Is Mr. Croft there at the station?"

The woman hesitated.

"I guess I could just wander around the lake and see if I can find him," I said, baiting the hook. The last thing the sheriff would want was another missing woman—even if it was just Rosella Midnight, the town circus freak. "Unless you think that would be too risky?" I prompted.

"Mr. Croft isn't here in the station," the woman said, falling hook, line, and sinker. "He's at the camp-grounds, following another tip. But please, ma'am, you shouldn't go looking for him. If you just—"

Click.

Tossing the phone into the passenger seat, I turned the key in my ignition and backed out of the Dragon's Gold parking lot.

The campgrounds were on the other side of the lake from most of the residences and businesses in town. Remote and peaceful, with breathtaking views of the lake and mountains. The family that owned the camp made sure everyone had access to the natural beauty of their property, offering various water activities, camping sites for RVs and tents, as well as a dozen or so cabins that could be rented. They also partnered with the local elementary school to offer the kids outdoor excursions and survival training weekends, along with a month long summer camp. The parents of Winterspell loved it because their kids could get all the benefits of summer camp while being only a few miles from home.

This time of year, though, the campgrounds were relatively deserted. A few people rented the cabins and did winter fishing or hunkered down for a romantic staycation, opting to spend their days hiking or going up into the hills to the natural hot spring. As I turned off at the campground, I saw the sign for the Winterspell Chalet that Jasmine had mentioned. The parking lot in front of it was littered with cars, and off to the far right side of the ski lodge–inspired resort, a trail of bike riders headed toward the tree line for a mountain bike excursion.

It hadn't yet begun to snow in Winterspell, which, despite its wintery name, only got about two months of snowfall, usually beginning in December. However, with the mountains surrounding the lake, there would be snow adventures within a short driving distance. I imagined that was what Jasmine had meant when she'd talked about snowshoeing and snowmobiling. The resort must offer some kind of transportation into the higher elevations when it wasn't quite cold enough to snow in Winterspell proper.

Turning off the highway into the campground's lot, I spotted two vehicles. The first was a black Ford truck with a twelve-foot trailer hitched to the back. On the other side of the lot, a blue station wagon was parked, its rear hatch open. Two twenty-something men stood at the back, one holding a leash that was attached to a border collie, while the other pulled a large backpack from the cargo area. I watched them for a few minutes before getting out of the car. They took off toward the trailhead, happily chatting, their breath making puffs of white in the frigid morning. At least they were dressed appropriately. Far too often, people fancying themselves as outdoorsy because they went on a shopping spree at R.E.I. wound up stranded on the hiking trails or lost after taking an unmarked path deeper into the woods.

Shutting the door to my own vehicle, I walked closer to the truck. No one was in the cab. "Shoot," I muttered, scanning the water. "Nothing like a wild goose chase in forty-degree weather."

Like the hikers, I'd bundled up, layering a North Face windbreaker over a fleece vest and long-sleeved thermal shirt. Still, the wind stung my cheeks and with my hair still partially damp, I wasn't going to be able to handle it for too long. Tugging on a knitted cap and gloves, I set off for the shoreline. A little ways down the beach there was a tall lifeguard and first aid hut. If I climbed up it, I'd have a better vantage point to see up and down the lakeshore. If nothing else, I could wait by the black truck. It had to belong to this *monster hunter*, unless he'd already left and headed back to the station.

A prickle of nerves crept up my throat and I scanned the shoreline once more. I'd warned Valkyrie to hide. She should be safe.

Unless Orion had some kind of power to draw her out.

My pulse quickened at the disturbing thought. I hadn't considered it before, but it made sense. My powers were unique, but there were other types of magic that enabled communication with animals. If Orion could reach her, would she listen and fall into his trap?

My heart sped up as I jogged to the lifeguard stand and hustled up the bleached wood stairs. A pair of binoculars was inside the unlocked hut, and I snagged them before taking a wide stance on the deck. Sweeping from the east to the west, I moved slowly, scanning every detail for any sign of the Order's hunter.

"What do you think you're doing?"

I about jumped out of my skin at the brusque voice. Lowering the binoculars, I peered over the railing and found myself staring down into a pair of obsidian eyes. "Looking for you," I told the cross-looking man.

Replacing the binoculars in the hut, I jogged back down the stairs and squared off with Orion Croft. He stood in the sand, his arms folded across his broad chest. He was dressed far more casually than the night before, a navy coat over a pair of black cargo pants. His shoulder-length hair was halfway pulled back, keeping it from whipping into his face with the breeze; all but a few strands the wind must have tugged free. He didn't look like the type to wear bobby pins.

"You were looking for me?" he asked.

"Yes. I have information. About the case," I replied, matching his hard stare as best I could.

His jet-black brows lifted. "Okay. Shoot."

I drew in a breath, weighing my options. How could I explain what I knew without giving away the source of the information?

Orion's brows lifted another centimeter.

"The sea serpent isn't responsible for these attacks," I said. "The warden has it all wrong, and I would be happy to take a meeting with her to explain what I know. But I came here today to ask that you hold off on your hunt until I can do so."

Orion's expression fell, clearly disappointed. "Well, that's not going to happen. Warden Quinton won't be returning to Winterspell until Thursday. Until then, she is unreachable, working on a classified mission for the Order."

Turning away, he started walking back toward his truck.

"Wait!" I called, chasing after him. "Please, you have to stop."

Orion barked a laugh. "Oh, yeah? And why is that?"

"I already told you. The serpent didn't do this. If you follow through with your *job*, you will be killing an innocent being!"

He went to the trailer and opened the garage-style door. One wall was covered by a weaponry rack, with two large trunks bolted to the floor beneath. The other side had a twin-sized bed and a small kitchenette, with a tiny fridge, patch of counter space, and a single-burner stove. He lived in this thing?

Orion strode to the end of the twelve-foot enclosure and grabbed a large curved sword from the rack. At his touch, the blade glowed faintly purple and I stumbled back half a step.

"You like?" he asked, flashing a half-cocked smile.

"No!" My heart slammed against my ribs, unable to convince my brain to stop looking at the weapons and envisioning the damage they might inflict. "Do you ... *enjoy* killing things?"

Orion shrugged. "It's not a matter of enjoyment. I was hired to do a job, and I'm doing it. It's as simple as that."

He considered my wide-eyed stare and agape mouth for a moment, then replaced the sword in its holder and sauntered back to the end of the trailer. "Huh. Usually the sight of my collection draws a more ... excited response."

"Excited about death and destruction?" I scoffed. "What kind of people do you usually hang out with?"

He cocked his head, his grin spreading. "I mainly prefer to spend my time in the company of beautiful women, such as yourself. But, I can see that you are different than the rest. Color me ... intrigued."

I blinked, snapping out of my temporary shock. "You're *hitting* on me? Really? I'm here, pleading for a creature's life, and you think waving a sword around and showing a little spark of magic is going to get me all hot and bothered? Ugh! I'd call you a pig, but every pig I've met has far better social skills."

Orion looked like I'd slapped him across the face. For a moment, I thought he was going to explode and start berating me. It was usually what happened when a woman shot down a man in such a harsh way.

Orion, instead, smiled even wider. "Okay, you have to tell me your name."

"I don't *have* to do anything," I snapped back.

He chuckled and held up a hand in surrender, before jumping back down to the asphalt to stand in front of me once again. "Fair enough. What is your name, please?" He arched one brow. "Better?"

I planted my hands on my hips. "This isn't a game, Orion—"

"Oh, please, call me Ryan. Orion is so … formal." He grinned again.

I know I shouldn't have noticed, but when he smiled wide enough, a dimpled cleft appeared on the right side and his dark eyes illuminated with a sparkle that seemed to glow from within. His eyes were so dark that from far away I'd thought them brown, almost black, but up close I could see specks of a smoky blue around the pupil. I'd never seen eyes that color before, the black and deep blue marbled together like something inside an agate stone.

Sighing, I let my hands slip from my waist. "Please,

Ryan, this is important. If I could just speak to the warden—"

"The warden isn't available," Orion interjected. "I wasn't lying to you. I can't even get ahold of her. She will return Thursday, and by then, I need to be prepared to hand over the carcass of this serpent. I'm sorry, Miss, but it's out of my hands."

Despair stabbed like a knife. There were two choices—reveal my secret to this virtual stranger, or walk away and hope Valkyrie could keep hidden until Thursday, when I could explain to the warden.

"What if—what if you can't find her?" I stammered.

"Her?" Orion's eyes narrowed, searching mine.

Crap!

"Or—or him, I mean. If they're hidden, and you can't find them in time—"

"Well, then it would be the first time in twelve years that I failed at my job," Orion replied, still eying me with skepticism. He reached down and adjusted the belt around his waist, and I noticed the various pouches and instruments hooked to it. Everything was black, blending in with his pants, but he appeared to have a travel-sized armory strapped to his hips. Great.

"The maintenance man here at the campgrounds thinks he saw it diving over near those caverns." He gestured toward a rock formation, below where the natural hot springs were located. "So, that's where I'm heading. Although, he did say there is a pretty romantic little hot springs near here. You might be able to distract me for a few hours ..."

Scowling, I crossed my arms. "Not a chance."

Orion shrugged. "Well, then, you'd better step back and let me get to work."

He heaved back into the trailer, grabbed the sword and a couple smaller knives, clipping them into his belt. Desperation squirmed inside my head, screaming at me to act.

Pressing my eyes closed, I said aloud the words I never wanted to admit.

"I'm cursed."

CHAPTER EIGHT

"*J*'m sorry. Did you just say that you're *cursed?*"

Nodding, I swallowed hard and opened my eyes. Orion stood before me, a half step back from where he'd stood before. Which, I supposed was fair. In our world, curses weren't something to mess around with.

"What kind of curse?"

Well, here goes nothing.

"I'm an elemental witch," I began, "and generally our power is thought to come from Mother Nature herself. She blessed certain lunar phases with different powers, in order to create a natural balance and order. Those of us born in the spring have earth magic, able to commune with nature to varying degrees. Some earth witches are gifted gardeners and farmers. Others have a special way with animals, skilled at training animals or healing them. Some earth magic presents on a more geological scale, the ability to conjure plant creatures or manipulate plant matter into other things.

"Witches and warlocks born in the winter have water magic. Again, it can present in several fashions: conjuring water, manipulating water, calling down rain, or even the ability to cast ice and frost with a simple spell. The summer is a time for fire magic. That one's pretty self-explanatory. Then, there's autumn magic, which presents as air magic. My sister, Jasmine, is an air witch. She can create wind and even cast small-scale tornados if she's really throwing a fit."

Orion listened intently, though I could almost feel the next question on the tip of his tongue. "And you are …?"

"I was born on March twenty-first, a day evenly split between winter and spring. Normally, this means the child will develop one of the two powers: water or earth. Sometimes, a truly gifted witch or warlock can wind up controlling two sets of powers. That's rare, but not unheard of." I drew in a breath. "However, on the day of my birth, there was also a lunar eclipse. It happened right as I was being born, and it's thought to have twisted my powers."

"Twisted how?" Orion asked, still studying me—though, to his credit, he looked less freaked-out than before.

"I can communicate with animals."

"How is that different than an earth witch? You just

117

said they can bond with animals and communicate with them?"

"Right. Some can, but it's not in the same way. See, when a gifted earth witch speaks with an animal, it's more of a one-way communication. The animals understand what she's saying, without needing training, and because of their spirit, the animals are more willing to listen. To trust. But at the end of the day, the witch has no power or dominion over the animals, and they aren't able to hear what the animal is saying in return, they can only gauge it by their actions."

"Okay ..."

"When I speak with an animal, I can hear what they are saying, as plainly as we're speaking now," I continued. "It's two-way communication, inside my head."

Orion nodded. "Okay, so you're Dr. Doolittle. That hardly sounds like a curse."

"There's more."

"Oh."

"If I want to, I can exert my magic over an animal ... sort of ... overriding their brain. It's like shifting, but my physical body doesn't change. I can send my consciousness into an animal's and see what they see, feel what they feel, hear what they hear. If I wanted, I could do truly terrible things, things against their will." I cringed, flinching away from the sickness that always accompanied the very idea of inflicting pain onto an animal.

When I reopened my eyes, Orion was staring at me, steadfast. "What about humans?"

"I've never tried," I told him bluntly. "And I won't. So long as I live. It's a vow I've made to myself—not to mention, to the Arcane Council."

Orion's expression rearranged; for a moment he looked almost impressed. "You've gone before the council?"

I shuddered at the memory. I'd been so young, and the spells they'd worked on me, testing and stretching my power—trying to find its limits.

"Wow." Orion breathed, rubbing at the back of his neck. "This is all legit? It's real?"

"Yes."

He frowned. "Who else knows about this? Does Sheriff Templeton know? Or, is this top-secret council business?"

I breathed a humorless laugh. "If only."

Orion canted his head, one brow arched.

"The entire town knows," I explained. "That's why that woman accosted me last night after the town meeting. She said I must be behind the attacks, that I must be controlling the sea serpent, and using it to lash out at the town."

"Someone said that to you?" He swore softly. "I didn't see you at the meeting last night. Leona whisked me away pretty quickly. Believe me, if I'd have seen you there, I would have remembered."

119

He grinned, the swagger and charm sliding effortlessly back into place.

A lone butterfly took flight through my stomach, but I quickly banished it back to wherever it had come from. Sure, Orion was handsome, but he also stood in stark opposition to everything I held dear.

"Why would someone think you were behind the attacks?" he asked, serious once more.

I scoffed, shaking my head. "I don't know. I guess, maybe they think I'm out for revenge, for the way they've all shunned me since I was a child."

"They're afraid of you."

It wasn't so much a question as a statement.

"Listen, I'm not trying to get your pity—"

"I don't pity you," Orion interrupted. "Quite the opposite. I think you're the most interesting woman I've ever met …" He let his words trail off, prompting me with a roll of his fingers.

"Rosella," I said, only a little begrudgingly. "Rosella Midnight. My mother's family were one half of the original founders of this town. The Winters and the Spellings."

"Aha. So, that's why you weren't driven out of town by pitchforks and torches." He said it in a teasing way, but it hit too close to home. If last night's little display was any kind of barometer, the angry cries of the villagers weren't too far off. The sooner I got out of here, the better. For everyone. Whether my family accepted it or not, I wasn't welcome here, and the longer I stayed, the harder it would become on all of them.

"Can you show me?"

I snapped out of my reveries and blinked. "Show you what?"

Orion gestured at the lake. "Show me your powers. Call up the serpent."

I folded my arms, giving him an incredulous look. "Oh, sure. You want me to tag and bag the poor thing, too? That sure would make your life a lot easier." Scoffing, I shook my head. "Unbelievable."

Orion chuckled. "Okay, okay. Fair enough. Something smaller then. There must be some tiny woodland creature out here you can do your Disney princess thing with."

Rolling my eyes, I started to object. I wasn't a circus performer. But then, I changed tactics. "I'll show you, but on one condition," I told him, extending my right hand. "If I can prove I'm not making this all up, you call off the hunt and help me figure out what really happened to Olivia, Amber, and Krystal."

Orion's jaw tensed, his smile extinguished. "I can't do that."

I dropped my hand and shrugged. "Okay, fine. Then, I guess we'll go with plan B. I'll just follow you around, like a shadow, for the next three days, ruining your hunt, until the warden comes back and I can explain it to her."

Orion's eyes sparked with a hint of anger. He knew

as well as I did how easy it would be to thwart him. The best hunter in the world couldn't go in for the kill if someone was there actively warning off the prey. "And what's to keep me from calling Sheriff Templeton and having him put you in a cell for the next three days?"

I hitched one shoulder. "He can't put my power in a cage. With a little time, I can have every animal in the whole forest on the lookout for you. With a little guidance, I'll bet they could prove to be even more irritating than me."

I expected him to shout, to throw a tantrum, or follow through and phone the sheriff.

Instead, he smiled. "All right, Rosella. You've got yourself a deal. You prove you're not making this all up, and I'll give you until Wednesday afternoon to prove everyone wrong and find a solid lead. Otherwise, I'll have no choice but to do my job."

He extended his hand. I took it.

"Deal."

Stepping back, I gave him a wary look before closing my eyes and concentrating. It was cold enough that most animals would be hunkered down in burrows and nests and dens. It took a little time, but after a handful of minutes of searching with whispers of magic, I located a small brown mouse living in one of the cabins. I asked it to help me, and the tiny little champion came out and ran in a figure eight for Orion. When it finished, it perched on hind legs and looked up at me, blinking. I thanked the little critter and broke off a small piece of the granola bar I'd found in the pocket of the coat. Leaving the mouse to his feast, we left the cabin.

"But how do I know you aren't just a normal earth witch?" Orion asked me, closing the door.

Sighing, I suggested another experiment. We wandered deeper into the woods and Orion used his tracking skills to find a rabbit's burrow. I convinced the sleepy bunny to come and help. I returned to the parking lot, leaving Orion with the rabbit in the woods. He picked out random items from his pocket, showing them only to the rabbit, who then telepathically told me what Orion was holding up, proving the communication went both ways. From a hundred feet away, I called out half a dozen items. When he emerged from the dense patch of conifers, he wore a stunned expression.

Which, admittedly, made me smile.

"Either you've got this whole forest trained, or you're the real deal." He rubbed his jaw.

"So, we have a deal?"

He nodded. "We have a deal."

"What will you tell the sheriff?" I asked, as we walked back to the truck.

He shrugged. "I don't plan on hanging around the station. I'll spend my days out here, in the woods. Biding my time."

I met his eyes. Could I trust him? Would he keep his word?

One thing was certain: if he broke it, I wouldn't stop until he paid for double-crossing me.

ON MY WAY out of the campground's driveway, I turned left instead of right. I wanted to get a closer look at the chalet resort. On top of that, I needed to think. I'd bought myself—and Valkyrie—some time, but not much. I had no idea what to do next, or where to begin. My journalistic training and years spent as a beat reporter gave me a few clear options; speak to the families, friends, retrace their steps. The majority of that legwork had already been done, but I couldn't go into the sheriff's office and demand to see the files. I'd have to work solely off of the information in the newspaper clippings I'd stashed in my room, and by speaking with those close to the victims. Which, again, was made tricky by my lack of officialness—oh, and the fact that there was a segment of the town that thought I was a mind-stealing freak.

Right.

A thick layer of fog enveloped me as I drove farther from town. I didn't have a destination in mind, content to just drive as I let my thoughts roll around, planning my next move.

It made sense to start with the joggers at the lake. It

was possible that some of the friendships extended outside of the niche group, and that some of them might have known the victims more personally. Besides that, after two days working in Sugar Shack, and getting reacquainted with all of my favorite treats, I could use a good run or two myself.

The question was, what would I do after that? I wasn't an investigator or a private eye. I didn't have my media credentials anymore—not that it was the kind of story a human paper would feature anyway, but still … at least that would be *something*.

All I could do was cross my fingers and—

"Ahh!"

From the fog a shape emerged. Gripping the wheel, I screamed and veered to the right. My car left the road, crashing into the thick underbrush along the highway. I slammed on the brakes, still screaming and swearing, but it was too late.

A *crunch* reverberated through the car and my chest met the airbag with a painful *thump*. Dust billowed up around me and for a frenzied moment, I mistook it for smoke and thought the crash had caused a fire. Panic surged through me before my rational brain yanked back the controls and realized it was debris from the airbags deploying.

I glanced in the rearview, just in time to watch the deer bound away in the opposite direction, unscathed.

"Sweet Mother," I whispered, sagging back, my chest heaving.

Gingerly, I started to open the driver's door. It was jammed, the frame crunched by the impact. After a few tries, I managed to shove it open. Adrenaline cloaked any pain as I stumbled away from the car, taking in the damage. The front end had crumpled into a twisted mess of metal. The windshield was cracked, but hadn't shattered.

In swerving to avoid the deer, I'd plowed over a few bushes and hit a tree. I shuddered to think what might have happened if the brush hadn't been there to slow my inertia. I tottered back a few more steps and sat on the stump of a tree that had likely been cut down long ago, to prevent branches falling onto the highway. My purse was still slung across my chest and with trembling fingers, I managed to find my cell phone.

As I scanned my contacts list, I debated who to call for help. I wasn't seriously injured, just bruised and shaken. I didn't need an ambulance or other first aid. The car was obviously toast. I'd be surprised if my insurance even agreed to pay for repairs. They'd likely call it totaled, write me a check—that wouldn't be enough to cover a replacement—and send me on my way with a warning to be more careful.

I tried Matty first. After all, we'd made tentative plans. When his voicemail clicked on, I hung up without leaving a message. Then I tried Jasmine. She too was unavailable.

"Great." I grumbled to myself and kept scrolling. Grandma Rose wasn't allowed to drive; neither was

Grandpa Gerald. My dad would come get me, but … I'd rather keep him from seeing the state of my car. That left … "Candice?"

Pulling a face, I dialed.

"Hey, sis," she answered on the third ring. "What's up?"

"Are you in town? I need someone to come pick me up. I got—I got in a wreck. My car's undriveable. I'm going to have to get a tow."

"Oh. Wow! Are you okay?"

"Yeah, just a little freaked." I rubbed my forehead. A headache was rolling in; I could feel it percolating behind my brows. "Can you come pick me up?"

"Hmm. I'm a little busy, but I can get you a ride." She spoke to someone in the background, though I couldn't make out the exact words. It sounded like she was explaining the whole thing to her friends.

"Where are you at?" she asked, coming back on the line.

"I'll text you the GPS coordinates. There aren't any good landmark nearby. I'm out past the Winterspell Chalet."

"Okie dokie. Hang tight."

"Cand—"

Beep beep beep.

Groaning, I dropped the phone into my lap. She hadn't said she would come and get me, just that she would get me a ride. After a moment, I checked my phone, seeing if either Jasmine or Matty had tried to call back.

Nothing.

Reluctantly, I texted the GPS location to Candice and then went back to the wreckage of my car. The rear hatch still opened. I had an emergency kit in the back, including a small first aid kit. I grabbed a bottle of water and a pack of acetaminophen for the headache.

I'd been a good half an hour from town when I crashed, so I settled back on the stump, took the meds, and guzzled half the bottle of water before pulling up a notes file on my phone. After typing up the next steps of my investigation, I did a quick internet search for local police reports. If women were missing from inside Winterspell, it was entirely possible they were missing from nearby non-magic towns. I went back a couple years, but was unable to find anything close to fitting the profile.

Deflated, I checked that item off my list.

A pair of headlights cut through the fog, and I scolded myself for underestimating Candice. She was young, but she could be responsible. She came through when it really counted.

Then I realized it wasn't Candice's cute little red coupe headed my way. It was a tow truck. Which, normally, would be a welcome sight following a bad car crash. But in this case, it was very much not.

Because, as the truck neared, I caught a glimpse of the driver, and my heart plummeted.

Behind the wheel sat Jake March.

He passed me by a couple yards and then pulled the tow truck off to the shoulder to park. It might have been my imagination, but it seemed to take him an extra minute to get out of the cab.

"Hey, El," he said, coming around the back, his hands stuffed in the pockets of oil-stained jeans. A ball cap was pulled low on his brow, hiding those storm-cloud gray eyes, which was probably for the best. I couldn't see them without also seeing the ghosts of our memories.

I stayed on the stump. Despite the painkillers, I was starting to feel the effects of the crash and didn't feel much like moving. "Hey, Jake. I guess Candice called you?"

He nodded, then planted his feet and surveyed the damage with a low whistle. "Wow." Glancing at me, he frowned. "You sure you're not hurt?"

I shrugged. "A little banged up. Nothing some ice and rest won't fix."

Not that I had time to rest.

"What happened?" he asked, going closer to inspect the vehicle.

"Deer ran out in front of me," I said. "Swerved to avoid hitting it, and …" I clucked my tongue. "Overreacted a little bit."

He considered me a moment longer. He knew I was

stubborn, and obviously didn't trust my own medical assessment.

"I'm fine," I said, groaning a little as I got to my feet. "You didn't have to come out here and get me."

Jake smiled and hooked a thumb at the tow truck. "It's kind of my gig."

Smiling, I bobbed my head. "Right, I just meant … you know, I could have gotten a ride into town and had you come out here later, or something."

Jake slipped his hands back into his pockets. "I don't mind, Ella. Honestly. Things between us … they don't have to be awkward, if we don't want them to be. All that stuff is in the past."

I nodded. Logically, I knew he was right, but there are some wounds that just don't heal all the way. No matter how much you want them to.

Wincing a little as I rolled my shoulders back, I wondered how bad the bruising would be across my chest from the impact of the seat belt and airbags. Although, if that was the worst of it, I was one lucky witch. "So, do you think you'll be able to get her out of here?"

Jake flashed me a quick smile. "I've seen much worse."

"Okay. And for the big-money question … is she totaled?"

Jake pulled a face and I had my answer. He was going to try and candy coat it, but the truth was there, plain as day. Groaning, I pressed my palms against my eyes. My brain launched into a mental accounting session, playing with invisible money. My parents would pay for my hours at Sugar Shack, and I didn't have to worry about rent this month ... but I needed to be saving for a deposit on my next place. First and last month's rent, plus a security deposit, and whatever crazy fee they wanted to charge for Karma ...

There was no way I could afford to buy another car. But without one, I was good and stuck. Stuck in Winterspell.

Jake was already moving. He set about putting out some emergency flares, a good fifty feet from the site, one in each lane, then set up some pop-up cones to help guide traffic around his truck. Finally, he had me stand off to the side and then climbed back in his truck, to maneuver it into position. I took refuge on my stump, watching as he backed in and started setting things up so he could tow the car by its back bumper. He used a control pad to slowly reel in the long hook he'd affixed to the underside of the car, pulling it free of the brush and shrubbery. When it was close enough, he shifted his equipment around and got the car hoisted up to pull behind his work truck.

When things were in place, he snuffed out the flares and collected the caution cones and put them back in one of the built-in toolboxes in the bed of the truck. He brushed his hands together and looked at me. "You got everything? I think we're ready to go, here."

"Oh. Right." I took one final look at the scene, then

headed for the passenger side. Jake stepped in and opened the door for me. I brushed past him as I climbed in, close enough to catch a whiff of his after-shave. *Mother help me.* It was the same one he'd worn in high school. Classics never go out of style, I guess. It was a fresh scent with sandalwood undertones. Of course, it now had an extra note of mechanic grease, but for whatever reason, that only made it more appealing.

Swallowing hard, I got in the passenger seat and buckled up. Jake climbed in behind the wheel, and we took off down the highway. The radio played a slow country song. Exhaling, I leaned my head back against the seat and closed my eyes. "I've always had awesome timing, haven't I?"

Jake chuckled softly. "You like to keep people guessing."

Rolling my head to one side, I considered his profile. It was good to see him smile. I'd never wished him ill, even though I found it impossible to imagine him being with someone else. I still wanted it for him, eventually. Looking at him now, a spark of curiosity grew, but I couldn't muster up the courage to ask him. It probably wasn't the right timing anyway.

"Thanks for coming to get me," I said. "Even if it is your job and all."

He smiled and glanced over at me. "You're welcome."

The song ended and the DJ came on, reading a scripted advertisement for a local barbecue joint.

"What's it like?" Jake asked, his eyes back on the road. "Being back, I mean. After all this time."

"Weird," I said flatly. "It's like nothing has changed, and yet, everything feels different. Which, I get, makes no sense whatsoever."

"Nah, it kind of does. I mean, it's your home, but you've also had a home elsewhere. And a bunch of us still live here, but we're all doing different things. You know? It still sort of blows my mind to watch our former classmates with their partners and kids. Last month, Tiffany Harper came in for an oil change. She's got three kids now!"

I whistled. "Who's the guy?"

Jake laughed. "Guess."

I scrunched up my nose. "Not Gentry."

"Bingo! He finally won her over," Jake said with a chuckle. "I guess they got together three years out of school. Settled down and got to work on building a family."

"Wow."

"The power of perseverance," he added, still grinning.

"Sometimes the nerd gets the prom queen," I added with a baffled smile. "Good for Gentry. Although, it might be more of a 'be careful what you wish for' thing. I was in choir with Tiffany the last three years of school. She's a handful and a half."

133

"I think that's what Gentry liked about her," Jake teased.

Without thinking, I thwapped him on the arm. It was like muscle memory. Something I'd done hundreds of times before, but this time, it felt all wrong. I yanked my hand back and muttered a quick apology. Jake didn't comment.

We drove in silence for a few miles, the radio the only distraction, though its volume was low enough that it was hard to make out the song lyrics. Someone probably singing about their lost dog or cheatin' ex. I'd never been a huge country music person. It was one thing Jake and I used to battle about before going on a road trip. We'd play rock, paper, scissors to see who got to pick the mix CD for the drive.

"So, besides the new business, what else have you been up to?" I asked.

"Oh, you know, the same old thing. I still like going on hikes. I did the Hood to Coast Relay, down in Oregon, last year. That was a lot of fun. I play pickup basketball at the community center on Wednesdays, hit the bar for a cold beer on a Friday night. Not much has changed."

"And you like having the shop?"

Jake smiled. "Yeah. It's been great. Business has been busy for everyone. Your family probably told you about the new vacation spot."

"Yeah. I drove by it, on my way up here."

"Oh, right." Jake glanced at me. "What are you doing

way out here anyway? Plotting your next escape? Cause you know they have this all locked up. Eventually, you would have just looped around and wound up back in town. There's nothing out here but some farmland and wildlife refuges."

When I didn't answer right away, he mistook my silence. Clearing his throat, he hitched one shoulder. "Not that it's any of my business, obviously."

"No, it's not that. It's just—" For a moment, I considered telling him the truth. Someone like Jake could prove to be a good ally, someone to back me up, and for all I knew, maybe he could even help with the investigation I was launching. He knew things going on in town; he had connections, access to people, and a more personable nature when it came to the locals.

But even if he agreed to help, it would just put us in closer contact with each other, and the twenty-minute drive was already proving to be somewhat awkward. He was right: what we had, it was in the past. And it was best it stayed there.

"I just needed to clear my head," I told him. "I didn't really have a destination in mind."

He appeared to buy it, but conversation ran dry after that, each of us seemingly retreating to our own corners. Jake dropped me off at my parents' house before driving the car back to his shop for a full assessment. He promised to call the next day with an update and even offered to help in dealing with my auto insurance company—seeing as they were a human-world organization and we were in no-man's-land.

"Thanks, again," I told him, when he helped me from the truck. "I appreciate it."

"Anytime," he said, then smiled. "But next time you want to say hi, just stop by Merlin's Well on a Friday."

I sputtered an objection, and he laughed as he jogged around the front of his truck and climbed back behind the wheel. He rolled down the window as he drove away. "Bye, El."

"Bye, Jake."

Turning, I started up the steps of my parents' front porch, and stopped short when I spotted three sets of eyeballs watching from the windows flanking the front door.

"Oh, for Mother's sake."

CHAPTER NINE

"This is all *very* mature," I complained, stepping inside to confront Grandma Rose, Jasmine, and Matty. Also known as, the three-headed peeper. "Seriously, it's not like we're in high school anymore."

"I'm sorry, but when you show up in the front seat of Jake March's truck, people are going to talk," Jasmine told me.

Matty nodded. "Which includes us."

"Also, was that your car, dragging from the back of the truck?" Jasmine asked, peering out through the sheer curtain to glance at the driveway.

"Yes. I tried calling both of you when it happened and got voicemail. So, really, we wouldn't even be having this conversation if you people answered your phones!"

Matty laughed and slung an arm around my shoulders. "Okay, okay. Calm down, El. We're just messing with you. I'm sorry about the car. Are you okay?"

"Yes. Just gonna have some bruises, I think." Gingerly, I walked toward the couch.

"I'll get you an ice pack. Mom keeps one in the freezer, ever since she sprained her ankle last year." Jasmine crossed through the living room, into the kitchen.

From the couch, I heard her open the freezer door. "Mom sprained her ankle?"

"Yeah." Jasmine came back into the living room, carrying a blue gel pack with a fine layer of frost on the outside. Handing it to me, she sat beside me, giving me a thorough once-over. "She bought dancing lessons, for her and Dad, to celebrate their anniversary. On their first lesson, they got tangled up—doing the tango of all things—and Mom ended up hitting the floor. She landed wrong and wound up in one of those walking boot things for a few weeks."

I blinked. No one had even called. I mean, it wasn't like she'd had a stroke or something, but still … it bothered me that no one thought to mention it.

"What happened with the car?" Matty asked, sitting beside me. His weight shifted the cushions and I turned, leaning against the arm of the sofa.

"Deer ran out in front of me."

Matty swore. "I'm glad you're okay."

"Thanks."

"Now, about Jake—"

I groaned.

"It's not going to help if you don't use it," Jasmine fussed, snatching the ice pack. "You've got a pretty nice red mark here, from the seat belt."

Without my coat and vest, the V-neck of my long-sleeved T-shirt revealed the top part of the seat belt–inflicted bruise. Jasmine grimaced as she applied the ice, as though her skin was also being burned by the cold pack. "Maybe we should take you to the clinic."

I waved her off. "No. I'm fine. I just need a minute."

"You're going to be sore tomorrow," Matty said. "Remember when I wrecked my mom's minivan senior year? Coach made me sit out wrestling practice for two weeks, said I was moving like an old lady."

"Hey!" Grandma Rose bristled as she carried a cup of tea into the living room. I hadn't even noticed her leave to go make it. "As an esteemed member of the old lady club, I'll have you know, I could take Coach Parker in a wrestling match. In fact, I saw him at the market, not three days ago. Lookin' like a keg with legs!"

Matty grinned. "I've missed you, Ms. Rose."

"Why, thank you, dear." She extended the cup toward me. "Here, Rosella, this will help with the pain."

"Thank you, Grandma, but honestly, I'm fine."

Grandma Rose's gentle smile vanished, her eyes turning into those of a stern substitute teacher with a class full of rowdy kids. "Just drink it."

"Yes, ma'am." I muttered, lifting the cup to my lips.

Matty's grin widened.

"Tell you what," he said, getting up from the couch, "I'll go over to Whimzee's and get us some lunch. Then we can put on a movie and chill here. The weather's turning nasty anyway."

"Thanks, Matty."

He took everyone's order, then bundled into his brown jacket and headed out into the cold.

"I don't know why the two of you never were a thing," Jasmine said, taking his place on the couch. "He's so sweet to you."

I shrugged. "We kissed once in middle school. He was my first, actually. But I'm not sure it counted." Giggling at the memory of the two of us, awkward little preteens fueled more by curiosity than emotion. "We love each other, but not in that way."

Jasmine shook her head. "Do you need anything else? An extra pillow?"

Karma marched into the room and jumped up into my lap, settling down instantly into a purring puddle.

Smiling, Jasmine stroked the cat's fur. "She's a real lovebug, huh?"

"I found her as a kitten in the breezeway behind my apartment building. I looked for hours, trying to find her siblings or her mother … but no luck. There was another mama cat in the neighborhood, and she agreed to take care of her. But when Karma was old enough to venture out on her own, she came back to me. I guess it was kind of meant to be."

Jasmine scratched the cat's chin. "She must be very

special. I can barely get Flotsam to pay any attention to me unless I have a saucer of tuna for him. He and Jetsam are total barn cats now; they like the chickens more than us people."

I laughed and then sipped at the tea. "Cats are funny little creatures."

Samantha—sensing she was losing her spotlight—came trotting in and nuzzled into Jasmine's leg. Laughing, she stroked the dog's face and ears. "That's why I'm a dog person. Isn't that right, girl?"

Samantha offered a big doggy grin, looking up at Jasmine with huge brown eyes of adoration.

I stroked Karma's chin. Personally, I'd never be able to choose. They were all special to me. No one else would understand me going to the mat for a sea serpent's life, but I'd come to accept that there were some things I couldn't explain to others, no matter how hard I tried. It was just part of the gig.

WHAT GRANDMA ROSE had left out was that in addition to pain relief, her special little tea blend also knocked me out like a punch from an elite prizefighter. When my eyes opened, the living room around me was dark but for two slivers of light where the porch lanterns' glow shone through the sidelight windows flanking the front door.

Disoriented, I rolled to my side, and my neck and

shoulders reminded me of the accident. Someone had taken away the ice pack and covered me with a blanket. They'd even tucked a pillow from my bed under my head. I was tempted to stay there and succumb back to sleep, but knew I'd be more comfortable in my own bed. I also really needed to use the bathroom. The last thing I remembered was petting Karma, talking with Jasmine. Then it dissolved into a familiar chatter of voices as I dozed off.

My stomach growled. I'd fallen asleep before Matty returned with the food. Gingerly, I walked into the kitchen and checked the fridge. Sure enough, there was a Whimzee's bag with my name written in Sharpie on the front. I carried it with me to my room, and after a quick pit stop in the bathroom, I propped myself up against the headboard and played a TV show on my phone while I ate the cold sandwich.

It was eleven thirty when the episode ended. I felt more awake, but fog still clouded the edges of my mind, making it hard to think straight. Flipping through my phone, I found the list of action items I'd drawn up while waiting for Jake. I needed to speak with the jogging group. Which meant, I needed to be up and ready by dawn. According to Jasmine, the group had different meeting times to work with various schedules, but the main segment ran first thing in the morning and met by the public restroom at the rest area, the same one I'd used that morning to change into my wet suit, though thinking about it, it seemed as though it had been days ago.

Tomorrow was Monday. I had two and a half—maybe three-quarters—days to find a lead in the investigation that didn't involve Valkyrie. With that in mind, I brushed my teeth, scrubbed away the tiny bits of makeup I'd worn, and climbed back into bed, my alarm set for four thirty.

The buzzing woke me on the first ring, my mind already swimming free of dreamland before the alarm went off. Groaning at the stiff pain in my neck and shoulders, I swung my legs out of bed, turned off the alarm, and did my best to stretch without agitating my muscles further. I didn't need makeup, but I swiped on some mascara to hide my pure white lashes after I pulled my hair back in a simple ponytail. Digging through my suitcase, I found a thick fleece headband and pulled it on. The band would keep my ears warm and prevent any flyaways from getting in my face while I ran—or shuffled, as the case might be. Next, I pulled on a pair of thick leggings, a thermal shirt, and another sweater over the top that could be peeled off once I warmed up.

Considering the accident, I wasn't after a heart-pumping workout. The more important thing was the pre- and post-conversation. My mission was to gather as much information as I could. Best case scenario, I'd unearth a clue to follow. Tugging on a pair of gloves, I slipped my phone into the zip-pocket on the leggings and headed out the door. The cold blasted me in the face like a cannon and it took every bit of resolve to march myself across the deserted street, down to the rest area parking lot.

I was the first to arrive, and for a moment I started to panic, thinking maybe I was too late, but then a car pulled into the lot and a pair of female joggers got out. Soon, another woman approached on foot, coming from the opposite direction as I had. The three exchanged pleasantries and started chatting near one of the park benches. A fourth woman came in a sleek sports car. She carried a dog leash in one hand, and a paper coffee cup in the other. Of the four, she was the flashiest in her attire; an all-pink tracksuit with a matching hat. Long dark hair flowed halfway down her back in what looked like freshly blown-out waves. She looked more like an athleisure model doing a photo shoot than a serious jogger. The dog she toted behind her was a puffy little ball of fur with stubby legs, trying desperately to sniff the grass as the woman strode ahead, jerking the leash repeatedly.

The four women chatted happily, clearly good friends. My nerves threatened to get the best of me as a small voice began trying to talk me out of approaching. I'd never been very good at making friends, especially when I had to initiate the first interaction. Here I was, a thirty-year-old woman, but suddenly it was like being in the high school cafeteria, watching the popular girls' table, wondering what they had that I didn't.

Screw that.

Squaring my shoulders, I slapped a pleasant smile on my face and walked up to the quartet. "Good morning, ladies. Mind if I join you?"

The four turned, smiling. "Sure!" the tallest of the four said. "I'm Tonya."

Tonya was about my height, with a heart-shaped face, fair skin. She wore her chestnut hair back in a tight French braid that hung to the middle of her shoulder blades.

The woman to her left stuck out a hand. "Claudette."

I took her hand and smiled. "Nice to meet you."

Claudette stood to Tonya's shoulder, a petite woman with a tiny frame. I couldn't imagine she weighed much more than a hundred pounds. She had sleek dark hair that hung in a straight pony down her back; a few strands stuck out from under her hat, a stark contrast to her porcelain skin.

Beside her, the woman in the pink tracksuit held up her hands, indicating they were full, but offered a smile. Up close, I realized she was a bit older than the other three women. She didn't look old by any means —and her body was in phenomenal shape—but I placed her in her late forties, early fifties, whereas the other three looked closer to my age, in their late twenties or early thirties. "I'm Linda," she said. "I like your headband."

"Oh, thanks. I like your dog. What's their name?"

145

Linda blinked, then glanced down, as if she'd almost forgotten all about the dog. "Oh, this is Fluffy."

How original.

"I'm Peyton," the fourth woman said. She'd been in the car with Tonya. She was a redhead, with a dash of freckles across a pert nose. Her hazel eyes were kind and warm, and I felt myself drawn to her.

"It's nice to meet all of you," I said. "My sister, Jasmine, said you all meet here to do a loop around the lake. I figured, with everything going on, it might be good for me to find a pack to run with."

Tonya blinked. "Jasmine? So, that means you're—"

"Rosella," I finished for her. "Yep. That's me."

"Oh, wow. I guess I didn't know you were back in town."

I laughed. "I convinced them not to publish it on the front-page news."

That seemed to cut through the momentary tension. The other four laughed politely. Tonya spoke again. "Well, you're more than welcome to run with us. We all keep a slightly different pace, so don't feel like you have to keep up. We just try to keep a buddy system, especially now ..." She cast an ominous look to the glass-like surface of the water. "I still can't believe there's this ... this *beast* in there. I had a nightmare, right after that town hall meeting. It's just so awful."

"Hopefully it's captured soon," Claudette agreed, but then a smile spread across her face. "Although, I wouldn't mind if that Orion stuck around a little longer."

Tonya and Peyton exchanged a scandalized—but entirely delighted—smirk. "He is pretty dreamy," Peyton agreed with a giggle.

"Seriously, where has the Order been hiding him?" Claudette demanded. "I'd feel much better if he was the one patrolling the streets, instead of that sloppy drunk, Templeton."

Linda threw back the last contents of her coffee cup and walked Fluffy over to throw the cup in the nearest trash can. When she came back, she jogged in place a little. "Okay, ladies. Let's hit it, before the coffee in my veins freezes and I turn into a cappuccino Popsicle."

The other three laughed and after a quick self-led stretching session, we took off. My pace was painfully slow. I was a three-times-a-week kind of jogger, but had been going out more often prior to my move, to help combat the stress. In the darkest parts of my depression, running had been my one release. So, as a strategy to cope, I'd upped my exercise during times of intense stress and burnout. It wasn't a silver bullet, of course, but it did seem to help. Even still, I was never going to be fit enough to run a marathon, and with the lingering pain from the car crash, I was moving at about half my regular speed.

Peyton hung with me, though I wasn't sure if it suited her pace, or if she felt bad for me and didn't want to leave me behind. Either way, I appreciated it.

Ahead of us, Linda tugged her poor dog along. Fluffy's short legs were no match for his owner's and often trailed behind, just as much as the leash would allow. Peyton noticed me and groaned. "None of us know why she brings him along. She says it's because it's the only time he would get any exercise, but if you ask me, that guy would be happier at home on the couch with a Milk-Bone."

I didn't have to use my magic to know that was true.

"Some people just shouldn't have pets," I said.

"I'd love to have a dog, but I work long hours," Peyton said.

"What do you do?"

"I'm a dental hygienist. I work over at the clinic on Sycamore Street. Been there about six years now."

"That's cool. Do you like it?"

Peyton bobbed her head. "Yeah. I love my job. Of course, having a three-day weekend every week doesn't hurt either. Although, it does mean putting in ten- and twelve-hour shifts to get to it."

Smiling, I tried to pick up my pace. As the blood pumped through my body, my muscles were starting to loosen. I might pay for it later, but I wanted to up my pulse a little more. "I was working for a newspaper, but it didn't work out. So, now I'm back here for a little while."

Peyton glanced at me. "Sorry it didn't work out."

"Thanks."

We jogged in silence for a little while. Linda, Claudette, and Tonya rounded the corner, crossing over into a section of the path carved out between thick foliage and trees, temporarily blocking them from our view.

"I'm pretty new to this whole running thing," Peyton told me. "I sit a lot, for work, and it was starting to show. Although part of me thinks I should just join a gym and do all of this on a treadmill."

"It's good you guys stick together in a group," I said. "For safety."

Peyton nodded, but there was something in the set of her jaw that gave me pause. "The others are great, but I do tend to get left behind," she told me after a moment. "My running partner was—"

She fell silent, pain showing in the faint lines around her eyes. "My old partner was Olivia, one of the missing women. She was a newbie, like me."

"Oh, Peyton. I'm so sorry."

"I've been holding out hope this whole time … thinking maybe she'd just left, you know, like the sheriff said in his original press release about the case. It didn't make sense. I mean, logically, who leaves town without saying anything, leaving all their stuff behind?"

I didn't know what to say, so I stayed quiet, letting her process her thoughts.

"Now, I guess at least we know what happened," Peyton said, her voice thick with emotion. "It's good to have closure and all that."

"I don't know how long I'll be in town, but I'm happy to be your running buddy, if you want," I offered, smiling at her as we rounded the corner and veered off the paved path, onto the packed dirt trail.

Peyton returned the smile. "Thanks, Rosella. That's nice of you. I'd like that." She wiped away a tear as we kept our plodding pace. "If it weren't for the Winter-spell Runners, I probably would have packed it in and quit running altogether. It's good accountability. We're friends, too. A couple times a week, we go for a coffee at Dragon's Gold after we wrap up. You're welcome to come, too."

"Thanks. I just might take you up on that offer."

We jogged the rest of the loop, running up a hillside trail that eventually wound back to our starting place. It was a good, long run, and while my upper body was still a little stiff and sore, my legs enjoyed the familiar rush. Afterward, we gathered back at the rest area to cool down and stretch out again. The sun was fully risen and I basked in the warm glow on my frozen cheeks.

"Anyone for Dragon's Gold today?" Peyton asked, glancing expectantly at me.

Tonya frowned and checked her watch. "Actually, I can't. I have an early client meeting today. Rain check?"

"Oh, sure." Peyton gestured at Tonya. "She's my ride back. But, see you tomorrow?"

I nodded. "I'll be here. Thanks, ladies, for letting me join up."

We exchanged goodbyes and went our separate ways. I stopped a few feet from the crosswalk leading back across the street, and turned to consider the lake. Disappointment stabbed at my chest. While it was great to have possibly made a new friend, I hadn't gleaned any kind of clues, or even the tiniest start of a clue. The entire day lay ahead of me, and I had no idea what to do next.

As I stood there, considering my next move, a huge shadow swooped overhead. An ear-piercing screech shattered the silence and I glanced up to see a red-tailed hawk perched on a branch of the large pine tree at the edge of the paved parking lot. The bird spotted me and craned its head to one side inquisitively.

An idea sparked, reigniting the tiny embers of hope.

CHAPTER TEN

I didn't need to round up a battalion of woodland creatures to harass Orion, as I'd threatened before we'd struck our bargain. Instead, I could round up a search party. Dozens of eyes were better than just my two, and could cover way more ground than I could on my own—especially now, with my stilted gait.

With a pulse of my magic, I reached out to the hawk and made contact. The bird flapped its wings, blinking and twisting its head back and forth as I quickly explained the situation and asked if they'd seen anything strange around the lake. It generally takes a few minutes to explain to an animal that I could under-stand them, but most of the animals in Winterspell were aware, on some deeper level, of the magic woven throughout the town.

This hawk in particular didn't seem to find me odd

at all, and swooped down to a lower branch to engage in the conversation.

"Have you seen anything strange happening around the lake?" I asked after telling the hawk about the missing women. *"Anyone stalking or following women around?"*

In the animal kingdom, there weren't proper equivalents for most human-types of violence, but stalking and hunting were familiar terms. The hawk dipped its head. *"There is a man in a cabin on the other side of the lake, and the whole forest despises him,"* he told me. *"He pollutes the lake, dumping trash and other human things in it, with no regard for the fish and frogs and other beings."*

"What kinds of human things?" I asked.

The hawk canted his head, as if thinking. Wild animals often didn't have the vocabulary of domesticated animals, or those who lived close enough to humans to learn more of our languages for items. After a moment, the bird gave a frustrated chirping sound, then dove from the branch and clasped his talons at my coat, then my hat. *"Things like these,"* he said, going back to his original perch.

"Clothing?" I said aloud. "They were dumping clothing into the lake?"

The hawk inclined his head. *"And burning, all hours of the night. Strange smelling fires."*

My heart seized. "Which cabin?" I asked. "Could you show me?"

The hawk's gaze drifted, his eyes becoming intense as a small bird streaked through the sky over the lake.

"No time now," he said, still watching the smaller bird. *"Follow the main road; it's the one nearest the waterfall trail, where the road turns to the west."*

Before I could press for more information, the bird took flight, soaring away on a hunt for breakfast.

Deflated, I watched the bird vanish in the distance. There was no way I could find him again. My best bet would be to find the cabin—and more importantly, who it belonged to. Although, it wasn't the best lead, given there were dozens of small fishing and hunting cabins scattered throughout the dense forest. Magic wielders weren't too picky about where they built their homes, because for every modern man-made invention, there was a magic equivalent. Electricity, running water, and other modern amenities were easy to come by, when a large chunk of the magic population could harness the power of the elements. Winterspell Lake was green before it was trendy.

Pondering where to begin, I wandered back to the house and took a long, hot shower. Jasmine cast a blast of air magic at my tresses, blowing them dry with the snap of her fingers—a perk I'd missed since moving out on my own. With dry hair, I quickly styled my locks into a fishtail braid, hanging it over one shoulder, before adding a touch of makeup to complete my daytime look.

Then, when my family members had scurried off to work and school, I slipped out the back door and wandered to the small red barn, Samantha and Karma in my wake. In the wintertime, the chickens stayed inside the barn. Once spring hit, they'd have free reign over the yard, helping pick bugs from my mother's vegetable garden, and assist in turning over the family compost pile. They were wonderful little helpers, and had quite big personalities to boot.

In keeping with our theme, they'd been named after fictional characters: Flora, Fauna, and Merryweather, the three fairies from *Sleeping Beauty*. Two gray-and-white cats greeted me at the door with skeptical looks. "Hello, Flotsam and Jetsam, long time no see." I pointed down at Karma. She was roughly half their size, sleek and thin, where they were fluffy and a little rough around the edges from their time in the barn. They were still well cared for, of course, but had a tough, alley-cat look in their eyes. "She's off-limits. Got it? Play nice, or you'll answer to me."

"You always were bossy," Flotsam said, swishing his tail as he turned away.

Jetsam gave Karma one more look and then turned tail and trotted away with his brother.

Rolling my eyes, I wheeled around the corner and opened the door into the chicken coop. "Good morning, ladies," I said, grabbing a handful of feed. Tossing it out to them, I smiled as the three began pecking at the ground. "Any idea where Tumnus is?"

"He's not back yet, dear," Flora, a classic yellow-and-red hen, told me.

Merryweather, a gray-and-black hen, shuffled

closer to my ankles and took a little peck at my leggings. *"Worms! We want worms!"*

"Stop that!" I barked.

"Woooorms!" Merryweather demanded, taking another peck.

Jumping back, I held out my hands. "I don't have any worms!"

Flora clucked. *"They keep them in that silver box over there."*

Turning, I saw a small mini fridge just outside the hen's stall. It hadn't been there last time I'd visited.

"Woooorms!" Merryweather cried, beginning to run in a circle around my feet.

Sighing, I went to the fridge, grabbed a can of live—ew—mealworms, and tossed a small handful to the ground. Merryweather dove in with a chorus of excited clucks.

"She's become quite single-minded," Fauna told me, before nabbing a worm for herself.

"I see that." I shook my head, watching the frenzy. Merryweather was acting more like a starving piranha than a gentle barnyard chicken. "And Tumnus?"

"He should be back soon; it's getting quite late," Flora told me.

"Oh."

Thump.

The three hens winced, peering across the barn. *"There he is,"* Fauna declared.

"Poor thing's lost most of his sight, but he insists on going

out every night," Flora explained. *"He misses that window nine times out of ten on his way back in."*

"See if you can talk some sense into him," Fauna added. *"He's a stubborn old goat. Well ... for an owl."*

"Will do. Thanks, ladies." I tossed another generous handful of feed, put the worm container back in the fridge, and then went to check on Tumnus.

A stack of hay bales was pushed up against the window, seemingly to soften the blow, when Tumnus, an ancient (in owl years) barn owl crashed through the opening, allowing him access to the warm interior of the barn. Tumnus had been with our family since I was fifteen. I'd found him injured in the woods and brought him home to my mother. Together, we'd nursed him back to health and released him back into the wild. However, after six weeks of pampering and round-the-clock care, Tumnus decided he'd rather become an honorary member of the Midnight family.

It was probably for the best. In the wild, barn owls had a grim lifespan of only a couple years, whereas in captivity they could live to be twenty. I don't know how old Tumnus was when I found him—he didn't know either; animals don't tend to think in terms of time the way humans do—but assuming he was one or two then, he'd be creeping up on twenty by now. He wasn't our pet, and we never forced him to stay, but he had a safe home with plenty of food and protection from the elements, so I wasn't surprised that he'd lived as long as he had. If failing eyesight was the worst of it, the old bird might still have a few years left in him.

Two onyx eyes peered up at me and blinked. *"Rosella, is that you?"*

Smiling, I nodded. "Hello, Tumnus. Are you all right?"

The owl was splayed across the hay bales, wings outstretched and ruffled. As if noticing for the first time, he righted himself and shook his head. *"Quite so. It's been so long. I've missed your singing during morning chores. As we all know, your mother is tone-deaf. Candice often sings while she works, but Rosella, none of the lyrics make a lick of sense!"*

Laughing, I nodded. "Kids these days, am I right?"

"Quite right!"

"Listen, Tumnus, as happy as I am to see you, I actually came to ask for a favor. If you're feeling up to it."

Tumnus straightened, tucking his wings at his side in a way that made me think of an old-time admiral preparing to rouse his troops with a soaring battle cry. *"Anything for you, my dear. I owe you my life!"*

I smiled. "You don't owe me anything, but I would appreciate the help," I told him, before explaining the situation. I relayed the information from the hawk, then asked, "Does that match anything you've seen on your rounds? There's only so many houses close enough to see from the water, but if I were to go door-to-door, it would still take a while."

Not to mention, it could also be dangerous.

"*It sounds like the Templeton's' cabin,*" Tumnus said when I finished. "*Will Templeton, I believe. If I'm not mistaken, it was this past spring when he moved in.*"

"Templeton?" I frowned. Sheriff Templeton and his wife had two daughters. Neither of them would have passed their name to their husbands, assuming either of them were married. Then there was Gregory Templeton, Winterspell's former sheriff, who'd passed the baton to his son, Samuel.

"*There was a woman with him, at first, but all they ever did was scream at one another. Quite awful.*"

"Could you show me the way?"

Tumnus cringed. "*Perhaps tomorrow, Rosella. I'm not quite sure I have it in me to make it all the way back there today. You must forgive me.*"

"Don't worry," I told him, my heart clenching at the pained look in the old owl's eyes. If I pushed him, he would take me, but I couldn't ask that of him. "I'll find the way."

"*Do be careful; they say he has an awful temper. Prone to taking a shotgun out at even a field mouse!*"

The owl's warning only spurred me on faster. Thanking him, I raced out of the barn and jogged back to the main house. Winterspell Lake had access to the internet, of course, but it had its challenges. Delivery drivers weren't going to get past the sentries guarding the bridge into town, and the USPS certainly didn't have a route through town. Several households kept post office boxes in the nearest non-magic town, opting to use them as a workaround in order to purchase things from online retailers.

As a journalist, I used the internet near constantly to look things up, pull contact information, official records, you name it. The problem with Winterspell—which I remembered half a second after I raced to my laptop—was I couldn't look up property records online and determine the address for the cabin in a non-magic database. As far as the non-magic humans knew, Winterspell didn't even exist. However, there were some perks to going old school in a small town. Everything was kept at the official records office, which was only a short drive from my parents' house.

The only problem was, I no longer had a car and my family members were all back to work today. My dad's ancient truck was in the garage, but it was still up on blocks. Matty would be at his job. Sonia, too. Jasmine was at the bakery, and while she likely didn't need her car, she would ask why I needed it and I didn't have a great answer. I couldn't get away with the "just going for a drive" line again, especially considering how the one yesterday had ended.

That left two options. One was unthinkable. The other, unwelcome, but my only real option.

Sighing, I pushed up from the bed and started to get dressed.

ORION'S black truck pulled into the rest area parking lot twenty minutes after I'd called to ask for a ride. We'd exchanged numbers the day before, and I asked him to meet me at the rest area to avoid another scene like yesterday, when Jake dropped me off. Sure, there wasn't a complicated backstory when it came to Orion, but in some ways, that would only create more questions.

"And here you said you wouldn't call," Orion teased as I climbed into the passenger seat. He was wearing his half-dimpled grin and I wanted to smack it off him.

"Yeah, yeah," I muttered, buckling my seat belt. "Just drive."

"You haven't told me where we're going," he said, still smiling.

"Right. You're not from here." I adjusted the heating vent, pointing it toward me instead of at Orion. "I need to go to the records office. I might have a lead in the case."

"That was quick."

He almost sounded a little impressed. Not that I cared, of course.

I gave him the rundown and then rattled off a series of directions. He pulled out of the rest area parking lot. "So, being Doctor Doolittle comes in handy in detective work, too," he mused. "You ever think of going to work for the Order? It seems like your unique skill set would come in quite handy. Or at least get consulting work. They pay through the nose for stuff like that."

"Is that what you do?" I asked him. "Consulting work?"

"Technically, yes. I'm not on the Order's payroll, but I also don't take on any other clients. At least not anymore."

"Why not?"

Orion's jaw tensed, pulsing in the muscles near his temple. "The Order has enough work to keep my busy."

"And you like this work? Hunting … killing?"

He glanced at me. I couldn't quite tell if the question irritated him or confused him. "I protect people, Rosella. That's my job, the same as any of the Agents of the Order. We keep magic from spilling into the human world. Or, in cases like this, we remove threats."

I opened my mouth to argue the point, but thought better of it.

"Most of what I do doesn't involve ending a life," Orion said, almost defensively. "The job before this was in a small coastal town in Mexico. A pair of winged horses crossed the border out of the protected land where their herd lives. If they'd run into non-magic humans … who knows what would have happened. I had to track them and return them to safety. The job before that, I was in Canada. There was some kind of plague making its way through a pack of wolves. It was magical in nature, making the wolves go berserk. I had to track and trap the creatures so the Order could study—and if at all possible, heal—them."

"That sounds … intense," I said.

"I know what you think of me," he said. "After you told me about your powers, it made sense."

"What did?"

"The look of hate in your eyes during that first conversation. You see me and think I'm some kind of destructive monster, killing and slaughtering my way across the country."

"Orion, I—"

He lifted a hand from the steering wheel. "It's fine. I get it. The gods know I have enough weapons in the back of my trailer to outfit a small army."

"I didn't mean to offend you," I said.

He glanced at me, then shifted his attention back to the road and rolled to a stop. "Left here?"

I nodded.

"What do you think about Sheriff Templeton?" Orion asked after he made the turn. "You think he's dirty?"

"I don't know what to think," I replied carefully. Orion might work for the Order, but right now, he was working with Sheriff Templeton and his deputies; I didn't need anything I said getting back to the sheriff's ear. "But if someone's dumping things, including clothing, into the lake and burning late into the night, I want to know why."

"Right." Orion's mouth formed a hard line. "We found women's clothing in the lake, as part of the warden's investigation."

I nodded, having already heard that piece of information from the warden at the town hall meeting. "What exactly was found? Jogging clothes?"

"No," he replied. "But we showed the clothing to those who knew the victims and they confirmed they were pieces the women owned. There was also a necklace, found on one of the rougher patches of off-road trail. It belonged to the second woman, Amber."

My stomach sank. That was a hard piece of evidence to ignore. Someone was snatching these women from the trail—

"Wait ..." I frowned. "Why would the necklace be on the running trail, if they weren't actually out jogging at the time they were taken?"

Orion glanced at me as we rolled to a stop before another intersection. "What do you mean?"

"You just said the articles of clothing found—and identified as belonging to the victims—weren't workout clothes. So, that would suggest they weren't jogging at the time of their abduction. And if that's the case, then why was one of their necklaces found on a running trail?"

The car behind us made a small, quick *honk*.

"Left," I said, still chewing on a new theory.

Orion made the turn. "Well, maybe it's unrelated. It's possible the necklace was lost prior to the abduction. I mean, people lose jewelry all the time."

"Was the clasp broken?" I asked.

Orion paused, as if trying to recall the image from

his memory. "I—I don't think so, but I'd have to inspect it closer to be sure."

"Will Sheriff Templeton let you do that?"

Orion hitched a shoulder. "I can't see why he wouldn't. I might not be an Agent of the Order, but I'm the closest thing to it as far as this case goes. The warden reassigned the other agents as soon as I was called in. The case has effectively been closed."

That wasn't good. If the Order wanted this case closed and shelved, it was going to take a lot to get them to open it back up again, even if I found a compelling lead. The only thing that might get them to consider it would be another missing woman. But by then, it would be too late for Valkyrie, not to mention another innocent victim.

I couldn't let that happen.

Orion seemed to be thinking along the same wavelength. When I pointed out the small records office, he pulled up along the curb, but didn't turn the engine off right away. He turned toward me, and his eyes intensified. "I don't know if you've heard, but the agency is swamped right now. They're trying to keep that information secret, but response times are getting longer and the wardens are being stretched thin. It's only a matter of time before the larger, magic-world media gets ahold of the story." He glanced out the windshield. "Something is going on. Some kind of storm is brewing. There've been too many weird cases. Like those wolves I told you about, up in Canada.

They haven't figured out who started the plague. Now there's a sea serpent in the middle of a lake, as though it fell from the sky?" He shook his head. "It doesn't make sense."

Valkyrie's words came back to me. *I was bred for battle. When it became clear I was not a good monster of war, I was dropped here.*

The serpent's presence in the lake wasn't some magical fluke. She'd been set loose there. Had someone done it on purpose? To cause havoc in Winterspell? Or was there something else going on? Something far more widespread.

I didn't know, but something churned in my gut. A warning.

"Come on," I said, more determined than before. I swung open my door and hopped out, ignoring the protests from my injured muscles.

The Winterspell records office was a small, rectangular building. A small desk sat at the front, and behind it were rows and rows of file cabinets that stretched from floor to ceiling. Behind the desk sat a fairy with electric purple hair, green wings, and hot pink wire-framed glasses. Fairies varied in size, from tiny Thumbelina-sized pixie sprites to dwarf-sized high-court fairies. The one sitting at the desk looked about the size of Karma when she stood on her hind legs to bat at a fly.

"Good morning," the fairy said, a gentle smile on her face. "It's good to see you, Rosella. I'd heard you were back in town. How have you been, dearie?"

"Hello, Petunia," I replied, returning her kind smile. "I'm well, thank you."

Petunia's crystalline blue eyes shifted to Orion, and it might have been my imagination, but they seemed to go a little wider and glow a little brighter. "Orion Croft!" The fairy ran a hand through her brightly hued waves. "Oh, it's a treat to meet you. I don't know if you remember, but you once rid Briarwood of a terrible scourge of locust. My family lives there, and on their behalf, I would like to thank you! You saved many pixie sprites!"

Orion inclined his head. "It was my pleasure. You have a beautiful homeland."

"Thank you!" Petunia fluttered her lashes. "That is so kind of you to say."

I gave her a moment of fawning, then cleared my throat, drawing her attention back to the matter at hand—and away from Orion's face. "Listen, Petunia, I was hoping you could help me with something. Seeing as I'm back in town, I'm hoping to find a quiet little lakeside cabin. Before I go see the Farrow brothers about a rental, I thought I'd narrow down my search area a little; you know how those two like to take people on a wild goose chase."

Petunia rolled her eyes. "Boy, do I ever! They must have shown Dale and me ten different homes before we finally got it through their thick heads that we wanted a three-bedroom with a view, not a studio on the main strip or a mini mansion on the other side of the lake! Imagine how long it would have taken me to fly to work from clear over there!"

I smiled. The Farrow brothers were the town's only real estate agents, and had a reputation for being ... a little thick.

"Exactly. Do you know where Will Templeton's cabin is?" I asked, going in for the kill with a sugar-sweet smile.

"Will Templeton?" Petunia lifted a tiny finger into the air. "Oh, the sheriff's nephew! Yes, yes. Let me see—"

With a flurry of green sparkles, she spun and whizzed down a bank of cabinets, muttering to herself as she searched.

Orion looked at me, one brow lifted.

I couldn't help a little self-satisfied grin.

Petunia came back a few minutes later, a piece of paper in her hands. Her glasses slid down her nose as she bent her head to read. "The Templeton cabin is on Willow Road. You know where that is, don't you, dearie?"

"Willow Road? Sure. Now, are there any other properties out there? I think that's just the area I was looking for. Such a beautiful patch of lakefront, don't you think?"

"Oh, indeed!" Petunia sailed back to the drawer she'd left open. I wasn't sure how everything was organized, but when she came back, she handed me a leaf of paper. "This property used to belong to the Coopers, but they put it up for sale last year when they moved away. It might still be available. It's just a few miles from the Templeton cabin, so I'd bet the view is just as nice."

"Thank you, Petunia. Can I borrow this?" I asked, holding the page. "So the Farrow brothers don't get … sidetracked."

Petunia laughed, the sound melodic and cheery. "Of course, dearie. Just bring it back to me when you can. It's my only copy."

"Of course!" Turning, I smiled back at the fairy. "Thanks again, Petunia!"

"Anytime. Enjoy your day."

We left the records office and hurried back to Orion's truck. Climbing in, I read the address aloud. "We should head there, then backtrack and we'll find the Templeton cabin."

"She was nice enough, you probably could have just asked for the Templeton address," Orion said, starting the engine.

"I could have, but that would have raised questions. Why would I need the address to the sheriff's nephew's cabin? People talk here in Winterspell. Petunia is a sweet lady, but something like that would have gone straight into the gossip generator. Now, I've given her a different piece of gossip instead, a much more benign morsel. Rosella Midnight looking to settle down in a remote cabin will still get tongues wagging, but no one will think it's strange. To be honest, most of the town would probably prefer it if I moved to an isolated cabin on the other side of the lake."

Orion cast me a strange look. "In there, the woman, she mentioned you'd recently come back to town. Where were you before?"

"I was in Portland, working for a newspaper. A non-magic newspaper."

"Did you like it?"

I nodded. "Most of the time, at least. I was trying to get a promotion to one of the editor desks, where I'd have more control and be able to write more."

"That's what you want to do? Be a writer?" He took the paper from where I'd laid it on the console between us and plugged the address into his GPS.

"I have a degree in journalism," I replied.

Orion smiled as he eased the truck away from the curb. "That's not what I asked, though. I asked if you want to be a writer."

I sighed. "I figured it was implied. Why would I go to all the trouble of getting a journalism degree if I didn't actually want to write?"

He chuckled. "Fair enough. So, then, what draws you to reporting work?"

For a moment, I considered telling him about my travel blog idea, but decided against it. That felt too personal, somehow. Too fragile. "I'd like to eventually dig into the more intense, investigative journalism stuff, you know, uncovering some big story and blowing it wide open. The kind of thing most journalists only dream about."

"Hmm. And you'd rather do this in the non-magic world?"

I breathed a dry laugh. "Yeah, let's just say the magic world wouldn't take too kindly to me poking around in their business twenty-four seven."

Orion shrugged. "I don't know about that. You did a good job back there, with the fairy at the records office."

I glanced down at the paper as he gestured toward it. "I guess so, but that was—"

"Don't sell yourself short, Rosella. You have a rare gift. You should use it."

Frowning, I exhaled. "I don't think you know me well enough to be giving me unsolicited career advice."

He chuckled. "I've touched a nerve. It wasn't my intention."

"You haven't touched anything," I shot back, growing grumpier by the second. I should have just called Matty and waited until he got off work. "Not all of us are lucky enough to stumble into a job where we get to travel around, saving the day, and wind up being lauded as a hero by a horde of adoring fans."

Orion smiled wider. "Believe it or not, I don't do this job for the occasional praise. And I didn't *stumble* into anything."

"Fine. Forget I said anything. But the bottom line is, you have your life, and I have mine, and in three days we can forget all about each other and move on. There's no need to impart some kind of sage words of wisdom. I've got things under control."

Except, I totally and one hundred percent did not.

"I don't know about that, Rosella—"

Frustration bubbled up and I started to argue.

Orion laughed, then cast me a dark, smoldering look. "I was going to say, I don't know that it will be easy to forget about you."

"Ugh. Spare me, Casanova. There are a dozen women in Winterspell that would fall at your feet if you so much as smiled at them, so maybe save that charm for them. I'm not interested."

"Maybe that's why I like you," he said, flashing that dimpled grin before shifting his focus back to the road.

My mouth hung open for a good ten seconds, as I flailed for the right reply. When I couldn't come up with something scathing, I clenched my jaw back together and glared out the windshield.

We were on the same road I'd been on the day before, even passing the place where I'd run off the road. Orion glanced over, just as we passed it, as though he somehow knew. After a quick scan, he returned his attention to the road ahead. At one point, a car up ahead of us stopped abruptly, flipping a crazy-late blinker. Orion slammed on the brakes, muttering a string of colorful curse words at the car. I yelped as my bruised chest mashed against the seat belt. It ran over the opposite shoulder, but the part in the center of my chest was on target and the impact flared up a sharp pain.

Orion snapped a glance at me, his eyes intense. "Are you all right? What happened?"

Gesturing at my chest, I grimaced. "I'm fine."

He narrowed his eyes. "Something happened yesterday, after we met. Your gait is a little off today ..."

Scowling, I growled at him. "Stop checking out my *gait*."

A touch of a smile graced his lips, but his eyes remained intense as they locked with mine. "What happened?"

"I ran off the road, hit a tree," I grumbled, adjusting the seat belt. "I've got a bruise and that sharp stop just kind of bothered it. I'm fine. Can we go?"

"That was you?" He thumbed toward the road at our backs. "I saw the skid marks and the damaged underbrush."

Stars, he was observant.

Nodding, I offered a wry smile. "Ta-da!"

"You should have told me. I would have been more careful," he said, sounding seriously distressed by the idea of having hurt me. It was almost sweet.

Almost.

"It's fine. Let's go. I'm kind of on a deadline, remember?"

Orion looked ready to argue, but then glanced away and continued down the highway.

CHAPTER ELEVEN

*W*e found Will Templeton's cabin a little after eleven. It matched the hawk's description, with a little babbling waterfall feeding into a creek just across the road from the entry to the patch of property. The driveway was empty, meaning the occupant of the home was likely out for the day. I wasn't sure if that was a good or bad thing. I wanted to speak with him about the fires and dumping, but at the same time, I doubted that confronting him directly, without evidence, would get me more than a nasty remark and a threat if I didn't get off his property. If Will Templeton was anything like his uncle, he had a short fuse and a real issue with those who tried to rock the boat.

Orion had parked the truck down the road, and we'd approached the house on foot. The cabin sat in a remote part of the lake, with no one around for miles.

On the way in, we'd passed the cabin the Coopers had listed for sale, and for one wild-hair moment, I actually thought it might not be a bad idea. Waking up and taking my coffee on the shore, listening to the wind through the trees and soft sounds of the creatures around me. Under different circumstances, I might have wandered along the creek and enjoyed the beauty of the little patch of property. I wasn't interested in a remote cabin life, but if I was, I imagined a place like this might be nice.

As much as I enjoyed my life in the city, full of conveniences and activities, I'd wound up driving to the coast or the mountains most free weekends anyway. Granted, I hadn't had a lot of them over the years; between school, part-time jobs, and working for the paper, it had been hard to strike a proper work-life balance. Portland was a nice place to live simply because it was halfway between the mountains and the sea. A beach day or a mountain adventure was only a couple hours' drive away.

"Well, what do you think?" Orion asked, coming to a stop beside me. "This the place?"

I nodded.

"Okay. Let's check the fire pit, see if there are signs of human remains."

He said it so casually, as though he'd merely suggested checking the mailbox for a letter. Was his line of work so full of death and destruction that he could say something like *check for human remains* with such a casual air?

I decided I didn't want to know.

He was already moving, so I fell into step behind him. Sure enough, as the hawk had described, there was a large fire pit not too far from the water's edge. Orion grabbed a stick and started poking through the ashes, his eyes intent. I hung back a couple steps, not sure I wanted to see whatever he might find. When he frowned, I moved in a bit closer. "What is it? Did you find something?"

He glanced up at me. "Yes and no."

Squatting down, I looked into the ashes. He gestured with the stick. "I think that's a button," he said, pointing at a small, half-melted blob. It sort of looked like it had once been a large button, maybe from the front of a wool coat. "There's a few different kinds of fibers in here. And what looks like a brooch or pin." He pointed at a small silver shape. It did look like a pin, metal cut in the shape of a dragonfly.

"I can see if any of the missing women had one like it," Orion told me, still picking through the ash and debris. "Looks like there was some plastic in here too, but I can't make out what it used to be."

"So, he's burning clothes *and* dumping them into the lake?" I shook my head. "That doesn't make any sense."

Orion continued prodding at the ashes, then declared, "No bones."

Pushing up to standing, I took a slow spin, considering the patch of front yard, the small shed, and the front facade of the house itself. The cabin wasn't large, maybe eight hundred square feet in total. Large enough to have a single bedroom and bathroom, while still having a separate living space. A small carport stood in front of the shed.

"Let's see if the shed is unlocked," I said, already walking toward it.

Gravel crunched behind me as Orion followed.

I found the door unlocked. Which seemed odd. If I were a crazed serial killer, wouldn't I bother to lock up the doors?

"Unlocked," Orion said, seemingly going through the same thought process.

The interior of the shed went back further than I'd expected, and I wondered if it was some kind of spell. One that had been added on after the fact, to allow more space in the existing structure. I had no idea what kind of magic Will Templeton possessed, but there were skilled magic workers—like my father—who could perform such upgrades to a house. Granted, they usually charged a hefty fee for such a large spell. It would take a hefty punch of magic to make something like this, and wouldn't have come cheap.

Before I could search for a light, one appeared ahead of me. Orion cast a blue orb of flames and sent it over my shoulder, floating to the center of the room like a glowing chandelier. He smiled when I glanced back at him. "Impressed?"

"Not yet," I said dryly, moving deeper into the shed. Metal racks lined both walls, and reminded me of my family's garage. Two bikes were mounted on one, toward the front, with a kayak hanging from the other side. The back of the shed looked like a workout station, with a squat rack and a bench. Huge metal plates were mounted on either side of the rack and half a dozen free weights lay scattered on the thick black pad that reminded me of the floors in my high school's wrestling gym, where I'd gone to watch Matty compete.

"Quite the setup," Orion commented. "This is all commercial-quality equipment."

A row of storage containers and boxes sat along the other wall. I opened a few and found mostly extra blankets, camping gear, a random assortment of fishing gadgets. "Nothing over here," I said, replacing the lid on a plastic storage container filled with extra batteries, light bulbs, lighters, and other random "junk drawer" items.

Planting my hands on my hips, I glanced up, wondering if the shed had a loft or attic space. A little hidey-hole where one might stash evidence of their terrible crimes.

"Let's go check the cabin," Orion said, backtracking to the door. "We don't know how much time we have."

I followed him out and he closed the door to the

SPRINKLES AND SEA SERPENTS

shed. A series of stepping stones led to the front door of the shed, and I wondered if there had once been a nice-looking patch of grass in front of the cabin. Maybe even a small garden on one side, where a few pieces of lumber lay discarded in a heap beside a pile of dirt.

It was almost like the cabin had sat empty for some time before Will moved in. What had Tumnus said? He'd arrived in town in the spring. Only a couple of months before Olivia went missing. And who was the woman Tumnus had mentioned? Was it one of the missing women? And if so, what had they been doing out at the cabin with Will?

Orion opened the front door of the cabin—also left unlocked—and we went inside. He'd snuffed out the orb of magic light in the garage, and we didn't need one in the cabin itself as we easily found a light switch. As I'd expected, it was a three-room space: one bedroom, one bathroom, and a combination living/dining/kitchen. It wasn't terribly clean, but it also wasn't filthy, rather somewhere in between. Dust lined the edges of the bookshelves and TV stand, but the kitchen counters—while cluttered—appeared to have recently been wiped down.

It was a simple space, with simple wood furnishings. A TV and couch in the living room, with a bookshelf. A circular table with three chairs. And one small section of countertop and cabinets that reminded me of a kitchenette in a hotel room. The appliances were old, nothing fancy or upgraded. Personally, I would have sprung for a fridge with an ice machine before sinking thousands of dollars into top-level gym equipment, but hey, that was just me.

"I'll check the bedroom," I offered, as Orion scanned the bookshelf.

The bedroom was small and cramped, a queen-sized bed dominating the majority of the real estate. A shabby dresser stood on the other wall, leaving only a narrow walkway between the two pieces of furniture. The room only had one window, with peeling paint around the frame. The bed was unmade, and discarded clothing littered the floor. Wrinkling my nose, I called out to the other room, "This place has a real *bachelor pad* vibe going on."

Orion chuckled and called back, "Not all bachelors are slobby pigs, Rosella."

I didn't bother correcting the misconception about pigs being messy.

"You'd be welcome to my humble abode anytime you'd like, to take a look for yourself," he added. I couldn't see him, but I could hear the smile in his voice.

"No thanks," I replied. "You can send me a postcard, if you really feel the need to prove your point."

Orion laughed.

I pulled open the closet and froze.

"O—Orion—"

Quick footsteps sounded as he hurried into the room. "What? What is it?"

With a shaky finger, I pointed up on the shelf. A banker box sat in the middle, wedged between a pile of knit sweaters and a stack of board games. A sticker was affixed to the front of the box, with the name Olivia written in black Sharpie.

Orion swore.

My pulse spiked as I reached for the box, only to have my heart plunge to the depths of my stomach when Orion grabbed my arms and hissed, "Stop!"

Gravel crunched under tires, audible through the front door, which we'd stupidly left wide open. Faster than lightning, Orion raced from the bedroom and closed the front door, then barreled back, slammed the closet shut, and hauled me around the waist, pushing me to the window. "Go!"

"But the box—"

"Rosella, not now. We can't be here. We don't know what he's capable of."

"But—"

He threw the window open, punched out the screen, and gave me a boost. I tumbled through, landing in the overgrown foliage that crept from the forest right up to the wood siding of the backside of the cabin. My neck and shoulders complained, but I got myself upright and scampered into the woods. Orion closed the window, replaced the screen, and hurried after me.

We stopped a hundred feet from the cabin to catch

our breaths. "That was close," Orion said, raking a hand through his dark hair.

"Now do you believe me?" I hissed. "It wasn't Valkyrie. She didn't kill those women!"

"Valkyrie is the serpent?"

"Yes."

He scrubbed a hand over his jaw, looking back in the direction of the cabin. "Come on. We need to get to my truck. We'll figure out what to do when we get back to town."

Exhaling a sigh of relief, I didn't even mind when he put a steadying hand on my waist as we picked our way through the thick underbrush.

WE MADE it back to the truck without anyone following us, though my heart rate only began to slow once we were on the highway and miles from the turnoff to Templeton's cabin. Swallowing, I glanced at Orion's profile. He'd gone steely. I doubted he would admit it, but the close call had spooked him, too. I'd seen it in his eyes. Though, I couldn't be sure if he was afraid of getting caught—or what he would have done if we had been.

Something told me I didn't want to know the answer.

"So, what now?" I asked. "Can you go to Sheriff Templeton? Or, try to get word to the warden? Or someone at the Order?"

"And tell them what? It's not like we found a body," he replied, not taking his eyes from the road. "We need more proof."

I huffed an exasperated sigh. "Well, I almost had it! But you knocked my arm away!"

"We don't know what was in that box, Rosella."

"Um, let's see, top suspect has a mystery box in his closet with the first victim's name on it; what could it be ... oh, you know, I'll bet it's where he keeps his left-over Christmas cards."

Orion made a growling sound low in his throat. "You know what I mean. We need more information. Something concrete. I'm not going to stake my career and reputation on a cardboard box and a little piece of tape." He cut a sharp glance at me. "Oh, and the word of a potential man-eating sea serpent."

I blinked. Where was all this hostility coming from? He'd been quiet but pleasant as we'd picked our way through the thick woods on the way back to his truck. So, what was the source of all this vitriol?

I was about to ask, when he grumbled to himself, something in another language.

"I'll go back tonight," he said tersely, not leaving it open for discussion. "I'll sneak in, when he's asleep, and I'll take the box."

"Are you serious?"

"Yes." He gave a quick, sure nod. "It's the only way. But if it's empty, or it turns out to be something else, then ... I'm not sure I can help you anymore."

"I feel like I'm missing something. Why are you so angry all of a sudden? When I called you this afternoon, asking for your help, you were all too eager to race over and pick me up. And you said it yourself, you don't have anything else to do until the warden returns. So, what gives?"

The muscles in his jaw flexed, his eyes hard as he stared at the road. "I wasn't thinking clearly," he said. "I didn't consider the risks."

"Well, that's not my fault," I spat back.

"I never said it was."

Things went quiet after that, each of us stuck in our own quagmire of self-doubt and irritation as our adrenaline levels crashed. Orion dropped me off at the rest area with a curt goodbye and he promised to call as soon as he knew anything. Part of me wanted to insist on tagging along for the stakeout, but then the idea of sitting in the cab of a truck with him for hours and hours, waiting on the sunset, alone in the woods … no. It was a bad idea. I couldn't identify the gravitational pull he had on me, but I knew it was dangerous and stupid.

Really, really stupid.

I'd just survived my second big heartbreak, and yet here I was, a swarm of hormones urging my heart to pick up arms and race into that war zone all over again.

It was still early enough in the day that I felt like doing something. If I went home, I'd most likely be alone, but for Grandpa Gerald, and he spent most of his time snoozing on the couch with a baseball game going in the background. I thought about going to Matty's and waiting for him to get home from work, then realized I had no idea where he lived anymore. Same thing with Sonia. I'd be better off texting and waiting for them to reply when they got off work for the day.

So, instead, I wandered up the street and walked through town. It was the first time I let myself stroll through the main street in a long time. In the past, I'd tended to dart in and out of the places I needed to do business, not lingering or staying out in public any longer than I had to. But today, I didn't care. The stares and whispers wouldn't faze me.

Most of the shops were brick buildings, lined up side by side with large window displays. A little produce market, an old-fashioned soda fountain and candy store, gift shops that catered to tourists, with Winterspell merchandise and other themed items. A handful of small restaurants, cafes, and of course Dragon's Gold Coffee, although I scurried past that one, not wanting to catch sight of my evil cousin Chloe.

I was perusing the window display at Glenda the Goode Witch's Dress Design, when a siren sounded. Turning, I found myself face-to-face with the sheriff of Winterspell ...

And Samuel Templeton looked thoroughly ticked off.

CHAPTER TWELVE

"*R*osella Midnight, you stop right there!"

Dread trickled down my spine, but I did as the sheriff asked—or, rather, demanded—and stopped walking. Sheriff Templeton got out of his marked car, slammed the door, and stalked toward me. He was average height, with a barrel chest and a belly that hung over his belt. He wore his official sheriff's hat, but I knew it concealed a balding head, and that the remaining wisps of hair matched that of his thick, silvery-white mustache.

"Afternoon, Sheriff Templeton," I said, wondering what exactly had his britches all tied up into knots. "Can I help you with something?"

He sneered at me, our eyes nearly level. "I should arrest you, right here and now, for trespassing on private property, and breaking and entering."

Oh, crap. Ice slid through my veins. How did he

know? Had Orion ratted me out? He'd gotten weird toward the end of our little escapade, but I didn't think he would have gone running to the sheriff. But then, I didn't really know him, did I? We'd only met some twenty-four hours ago.

Stupid. Stupid. Stupid.

"Do you deny it?" Sheriff Templeton asked, his brown eyes narrowed.

There were only two ways to play this: feign innocence, or go on the offensive.

I chose option B.

Slamming my hands on my hips, I leaned closer instead of away, and narrowed my eyes right back at the sheriff. All traffic on the sidewalks lining either side of the street screeched to a halt, watching the showdown. Even the cars in the road had stopped, though that could have been because the sheriff, in his hurry to confront me, had left his vehicle partially blocking one lane.

"Do you know why your nephew has been burning clothing and a woman's brooch in a bonfire outside his cabin? Or why he would have a box in his closet with the name *Olivia* on it? Is that why you haven't been throwing the full weight of your department at these cases? Because you know the truth about Will and are desperate to protect him? After all, he's family."

The sheriff's jaw went hard as granite, and for a brief moment, I thought he was about to smack me— or, at least, smack cuffs around my wrists.

However, the clusters of spectators were watching, and I'd just planted a few very dark questions in their minds. Questions the sheriff would have to answer. If he hauled me away now, he'd just look guilty.

"You just got back to town four days ago, and suddenly you know everything," he growled. "Is that it, Rosella?"

"I never claimed to know everything, but from what I've seen and heard, it looks like you've spent more energy coming down here to yell at me than you've spent looking for these missing women!"

"That's enough!" he spat. "You will *not* try and tarnish the reputation of me and my deputies with these lies."

"Then tell me the truth," I said. "Why is Will dumping things into the lake, burning other things, and keeping boxes of things hidden in his closet with one of the victim's names?"

"Olivia *Templeton* is Will's estranged wife," the sheriff said through clenched teeth. "Will moved into that cabin when they split up. They've been hot and cold these past months, and yes, in the heat of an argument, Will set about to destroy some of her things. Olivia called me, and I came out to defuse the situation. I spoke with Will and he agreed to stop the destruction. I don't know about a box in the closet. It's not really any of my business, which means it is certainly none of yours!"

He directed the last line to the spectators and a few

people took the hint and started moving on with their afternoon.

Narrowing his eyes even further, he leaned in. "The only reason I'm not throwing you in a cell is because the warden's liaison is taking the fall. He says it was his idea to go out there and search, and you happened to be available to show him the way. Now, I don't have to be a detective to know that's a load of horse droppings, but I can't prove it, and I don't want trouble with Warden Quinton, so I'm letting you off with a warning. But if you so much as step one little pinky toe on my nephew's property again, I'll gladly toss you behind bars. Is that quite clear, Ms. Midnight?"

I balked. Orion had been the one to bail me out of trouble?

Nodding, I cleared my throat, suddenly feeling like a small child. I'd let my bottled-up frustration from everything that had happened in the last weeks get the best of me, and it splashed out onto the sheriff.

"Yes, Sheriff Templeton," I said. "I'm sorry for trespassing. It won't happen again."

He eyed me, as if scanning for any sign of sarcasm, then gave a curt nod and stormed back to his car. He stuffed himself back behind the wheel—scowling at me the whole time—then whipped his vehicle around and sped off in the opposite direction.

My ADRENALINE WAS STILL BUZZING from the confrontation with Sheriff Templeton by the time I walked back to my parents' house. Not only had I just let my emotions get the best of me—something I hated, it made me feel weak—but I'd just made a powerful enemy. On top of that, I'd lost my only solid lead. Essentially, I was back to square one with the investigation, and no longer had an alternative narrative to offer to the warden when she returned and demanded to know why the sea serpent was still alive.

The house was still quiet, so I went to my room and flopped on my bed. Karma hadn't been there to greet me at the door, and for a moment, I worried she might have gotten into it with Flotsam and Jetsam out in the barn, but before I could go look, she came trotting into the room, offering a happy trill.

"Having fun out in the barn?" I asked.

"Oh, yes. The other kitties are teaching me to hunt mice!"

"Wonderful." Grimacing, I rolled to one side and scratched her chin. "Just remember, if they tell you the humans like if you bring your *prize* in the house to show off, they're lying. Got it?"

Karma tilted her head, but then gave a slow blink.

My phone buzzed against the bedside table and I lazily slapped a hand out to retrieve it, figuring it was Matty or Jasmine wondering what I was up to for the evening. Which was a good question. How could I go out to dinner or sit through a movie marathon at

Matty's, knowing that the grains of sand in Valkyrie's hourglass were running low?

The name on the phone wasn't Matty or Jasmine, though. It was Orion. Or, Ryan, as he'd entered it.

Eagerly, I answered. "Hello?"

"Where are you?"

"My bedroom." As soon as I said it, I mentally slapped myself and waited for him to offer a sly innuendo.

"We need to talk," he said, all business.

"I already know about the ex-wife," I replied, exhaling as I rolled onto my back and stared up at the ceiling. "I just had a run-in with Sheriff Templeton."

"He wanted your head on a pike," Orion said. "Glad to hear you're still breathing."

A wry smile crossed my lips. "I have a feeling I haven't heard the last of it, but for now, I'm good. Thank you for taking the fall. You didn't have to do that."

"It's not a big deal," he replied. "What's the next move?"

Frowning, I pushed up to sitting against the two pillows. "What do you mean?"

"To find whoever did this," Orion said. "You're not giving up, are you?"

"Well ... no, but—"

"Rosella, you dragged me into this," he interrupted. "I'm not going to walk away now. We just need to get smarter. What we did today, it was too reckless. Too impulsive. So, let's get dinner and talk. We both missed lunch, and I'm starving. You must know what's good to eat around here."

I chewed my lower lip. Dinner with Orion—in public—would certainly set the gossip grapevine abuzz. But then, maybe that wasn't such a bad thing, considering the current hot-off-the-press gossip would be about my smackdown with the sheriff in the town square.

Squeezing my eyes closed, I took the leap. "Okay. Dinner sounds good. I'll meet you where we did this morning."

"What are you hiding?" Orion asked, a teasing edge back in his voice. "I can't meet your family? Are they bloodthirsty trolls or something?"

I laughed. I couldn't help it. "No! They're not trolls."

"Then why can't I come pick you up from your house? Why all the cloak-and-dagger stuff?"

Karma glanced up at me, her eyes curious. I shrugged at her, as if she would understand. "You're acting like this is a date," I said to Orion.

He chuckled. "First of all, if I were taking you on a date, I would pick the place. Second, we wouldn't spend the meal discussing potential serial killers. And third, I would pay, something I have no intention of doing tonight."

I could hear the smile in his voice. And found myself smiling back.

Curse him.

193

He was too slick. Too smooth. Too good at drawing me out from underneath my grumpy little cluster of rain clouds.

"Fine," I said. "You may pick me up. And we will go Dutch."

Orion laughed. "I was mainly kidding about that last part, you know. We'll say dinner is on the Order's dime tonight."

That I liked even better.

I gave him the address and he agreed to give me half an hour lead time. We hung up and I changed into a merlot-colored long-sleeve shirt, added a delicate gold bar necklace, and swapped my faded, comfy jeans for a pair of more fitted ones with a darker wash. A pair of ankle boots, a quick spritz of hair spray to tame the flyaways in my long braid, and I was set to go.

It might not have been a date, but there was no reason to go out looking like I'd crawled through a half mile of underbrush.

Orion arrived right on time, and to my relief, neither of my sisters was around to play a quick game of Twenty Questions: Mystery Man Edition, before we could get out the door. Mom was in the middle of making dinner when he arrived, and while she stopped to introduce herself—and shoot me a quizzical glance —we made it to his truck without any drama.

"This is a nice house," he commented as we climbed into the cab. "You grew up here?"

I nodded. "They've added on a little over the years.

The workshop is relatively new. My father and grand-mother work out there, doing charm work, mainly. My dad likes to take everyday household objects and enchant them to be a little more functional."

"Sounds interesting," Orion said. "Does he ever do anything with weapons?"

Frowning, I buckled my seat belt. "No, and it's probably for the best we keep it that way. Knowing my Grandma Rose, she'd insist on testing them all out for herself and someone would end up missing an eye."

Orion chuckled and turned over the engine. "Sounds like my kind of lady."

"Well, she's single," I told him, flashing a grin. "I can get you her number."

Orion shot me an amused look, his dark eyes sparkling. "That so? Well, if you think I could keep up with her ..."

I burst out laughing, no longer able to contain it. And stars, it felt good. The past two weeks had been so stressful and dark. Old wounds and frustrations crashing together, leading me to the one place I swore I'd never wind up again. And now, ironically, a monster hunter was the silver lining.

Mother Nature has a twisted sense of humor.

"How do you feel about curry?" I asked.

"So, you believe the sheriff's story?" Orion asked once we settled into a booth at Elephant's Palace, a small Indian restaurant on the main strip through town.

Reluctantly, I nodded. "I asked my mom about it when she got home. Will and Olivia Templeton got married in 2013, here in Winterspell. They lived here for a few years, then moved away. Will returned recently, after the split. The cabin's been in the family for a couple decades, used mainly as a fishing retreat or a place to stash out-of-town guests that come in for the holidays."

"Your mom knows a lot about this town," Orion said.

I smiled. "That's just how it is here. Everyone knows everything about everyone."

"That's why you ran away?"

Wrinkling my nose, I leveled him with a stare. "I was twenty-three. That's hardly *running away*."

Orion shrugged one shoulder. I'd noticed he'd dressed up a little for the not-a-date, too. He looked more like he had at the town hall meeting, in a charcoal sweater and a pair of dark jeans. His hair was partially pulled back, out of his face. "That's why you left, though?"

"Well, that and the whole 'half the town thinks I can crack into their brain's hard-wiring and bend their psyches to my will' thing."

One corner of his mouth curved into a smile. "Right."

Our server, an Indian American woman with a warm smile and slight figure, came to present us with a basket of naan bread. When she left, I reached for a piece at the same moment as Orion and our knuckles brushed. He immediately pulled back, gesturing for me to go ahead, but the buzz of the soft contact lingered.

Stars, Rosella, what is this, high school? Get a grip.

"What about you?" I asked. "Where's home?"

I could equally picture Orion at home in a rustic cabin or some slick condo in the city. He was something of an enigma. Or maybe a chameleon, able to blend to fit his surroundings. Which left me wondering, which version was the true one?

"I have an apartment in Bay Harbor," he replied, tearing off a piece of the warm bread. "That's the magical community right outside the Bay Area, where the agency is headquartered. They like me to report on my cases in person when I complete a job, so the Bay Harbor community makes for a convenient crash pad."

I'd never been, but it was one of the largest secret magical communities in the world, population-wise. Compared to Winterspell Lake, it was a proper city, with tall buildings and a more compact footprint. The sheer volume of magic needed to keep it concealed from the non-magical world was mind-boggling.

"I end up spending some three hundred days of the year on the road, though," Orion continued.

I blinked. "That's intense."

He laughed. "It's not all work. I take four weeks off

per year: two weeks in the summer and two in the winter."

"Where do you go?"

"It varies." He took a bite, chewing it thoughtfully. "This year, I did my summer vacation in Tulum, Mexico. Tried the whole beach-bum thing on for size, took some surfing lessons, drank way too much tequila." He laughed. "It was fun."

I couldn't even remember the last true vacation I'd taken. When I was engaged to Leo, we'd talked about going to Italy for our honeymoon. All of our extra money went toward saving up for the doomed trip. When we split up, I'd needed my half of the pot to pay for a security deposit and other fees on my own apartment. There wasn't a lot left over for a vacation fund.

"What about this winter?" I asked. "What's the big plan? More sun and sand?"

Orion sipped his water, then shook his head. "I don't know yet. I was supposed to go visit my dad in London, but that ... fell through."

Something about the look in his eyes told me not to ask what had happened. "I guess you have time to decide," I said, offering a smile.

"What about you?" he asked. "You staying put? Looks like you've got a job lined up here."

I glanced up.

"I saw you," he explained, "through the window at the bakery, right when I got into town Saturday. I was getting some lunch at the place next door."

It must have been when I was with Matty and Sonia, sitting at one of the tables near the windows. I'd spent the rest of the shift in the back, or down in the break room. He'd noticed me?

My cheeks warmed, and I hurried to stuff a bite of naan into my mouth before I said something dumb.

His eyes glowed. He seemed to like tipping me off balance.

"I don't know—" I said, swallowing a little too hard. "I've been applying for other things, but nothing has panned out. I might just stay here a couple of months, save up some money, and then get back to the city."

"Portland?"

"Yeah."

"I'll bet your friends miss you," Orion said.

The question wasn't meant as a barb, but it pricked at me all the same. The truth was, I didn't have many friends in Portland. I had coworkers I occasionally went out with after work, or acquaintances I could go to when I needed help with a story. I knew and liked my editor and the others in the department, but I'd only ever kept them at arm's length. Thinking about it now, I wasn't sure why. I hadn't wanted to return to Winterspell, but still wound up resisting the urge to put down roots anywhere else.

Then there was Leo. That was complicated and messy ... and painful. He was a walking memory of what my life could have been like. If I hadn't been so ... *me*.

Nodding, I pushed a stray wisp of hair away from my forehead. "It will be good to get back. You'll have to look me up, you know, if you're ever in Oregon, busting Bigfoot or whatever."

Orion smiled. "I'll do that."

Our server appeared with our entrees and for a while the conversation lightened, as we talked about the food and tried one another's meals.

Toward the end of the meal, we rounded back to where it began. "Tomorrow, I think I'll head to the *Winterspell Gazette* office. They should allow access to the past articles about the case. I might even see if I can sit down with the lead reporter. Maybe they know something off-the-record that can help."

Orion nodded. "Sounds solid."

"What about you? How ticked off is the sheriff at you?" I cringed.

"It doesn't matter," he replied. "He doesn't have any sway over me."

"Will the warden be upset when she hears?"

Orion shrugged off the question. "The agency can't afford to get rid of me, so her feelings about how I do my job are somewhat irrelevant. At the end of the day, all that matters is that I get results … and I do."

"Right." I glanced down at my plate and picked up a scoop of curry with the flatbread. "How did anyone even know we were there? We were clear of the house before the truck's engine shut off. There's no way he saw us."

"Security cameras," Orion explained. "Sheriff Templeton showed me the footage when he confronted me at the station. Claimed his nephew set them out to watch for bears, but I think it might be more that he feared revenge after his little tantrum against the soon-to-be-ex-missus."

"Aha."

"He's got them well hidden," Orion commented. "I didn't see them when we were poking around."

Sighing, I finished the last bite, then pushed my plate away. "Hopefully tomorrow will turn up a lead." I glanced up, considering Orion. "Thanks for trying to help me today. It was nice to have someone watching my back."

Orion smiled, wiping his fingers off on a maroon-colored linen napkin. "Of course. I think you're on your own at the paper tomorrow. I can't explain away another day spent off the hunt."

The word echoed through my head, ugly and looming.

"Rosella," Orion said, drawing my attention back to him, "I'll hold off as long as I can, but I got word from the agency, my next assignment is cued up. I have to leave Thursday afternoon."

"I understand."

Orion paid the check and we left the small restaurant. He insisted on taking the long route back to the truck, and we wound up passing by Sugar Shack. The lights were still on inside, though it was just past closing time. Stopping in front of the illuminated sign, he grinned at me. "You know, I haven't had a chance to stop in here yet. What do you recommend?"

"The butterscotch chip cookies and the cinnamon raisin swirl bread," I answered on autopilot.

He started up the stone steps.

"Hate to break it to you, but they're closed," I said, gesturing at the closed sign hanging in the corner of the right-hand side window.

Grinning, Orion turned back to me. "Good thing I know the owner's daughter then?"

A cookie did sound good ….

"Okay, fine, but only because you saved my butt today," I said, joining him on the steps.

CHAPTER THIRTEEN

efore going to the paper, I decided to take a jog again the following morning. I was first to arrive at the lakefront rest area, and for a moment, as I bobbed on my toes and rubbed my hands together to stay warm, I wondered if I'd shown up on an off day. Then, a red sports car pulled into the small lot, and Linda and Fluffy climbed out. The woman spotted me and offered a wave before jogging over to join me on the sidewalk. "You're an early worm today, aren't you?"

"You mean early *bird*?" I asked with a laugh.

Linda thought about it for a second, then laughed and pointed at her head. "Right! I had a late night, guess I'm not firing with all cylinders today."

She was the kind to wear a full face of makeup out for a run, but even through the makeup, I saw shadows under her eyes. "I woke up late and didn't even have time to make a coffee before racing over here," she explained. "Hopefully, I can talk the others into going to Dragon's Gold after this morning's training. You're more than welcome to join, too, you know. The more the merrier!"

"Thank you. I just might do that." Cousin Chloe wouldn't confront me if I was with others, so I could put that showdown off for another day. And the *Gazette*'s office wouldn't open until nine, so I would have plenty of time to kill.

"So, um, how long have you been a runner?" I asked, still bouncing slightly to keep my body moving.

"Oh, it's more of a hobby for me," Linda replied. "I work long hours, and don't have much of a social life. The running club is a great way to get to know different kinds of people."

"Yeah. It is nice," I agreed. "Do you come every day?"

"Mostly," she said, wiping a strand of hair out of her mouth as the wind whipped her long ponytail into her face. "You have to be pretty dedicated to come out in this!"

We shared a laugh.

Beside her, Fluffy stood, bracing himself against the wind between our legs. His long white fur danced in the air like one of those inflatable used car lot balloon men, whipping every which way as he tried to find the best place to stand.

"Fluffy is my fur baby," Linda said, following my stare down to the dog. "We go everywhere together. He actually belonged to my daughter. I was never much of an animal person. But, well … she passed away two years ago, and I was the only one who could take Fluffy."

"Oh, wow. I'm so sorry to hear that." My heart wrenched for the woman. I wasn't a mother, but even still, I knew that had to be one of the worst kinds of pain imaginable.

"Thank you." Linda nodded, her eyes glossy. "She was a wonderful person. I'd do anything to get her back again."

"I'm sure."

"Heya!" a chipper voice called from the sidewalk. Claudette came into view, smiling broadly as she approached.

Linda brightened and I was grateful for the distraction. "Morning."

"Rosella, it's nice to see you back again," Claudette said, offering Linda a side-hug.

"Thanks."

Tonya pulled up a few minutes later with Peyton in the passenger seat. They scurried over, apologizing profusely for their tardiness. We started stretching and warming up for the run. Peyton came to stand beside me and elbowed me. "Nice work scoring a date with Mr. Hottie Monster Hunter," she said, grinning widely.

Claudette gasped. "What?"

Freakin' Winterspell.

"It wasn't a date," I said.

Claudette pouted, clearly not buying it.

"Word on the street is you two had an intimate dinner for two, sharing your food, and then went for an after-hours sweet treat," Peyton said, making goo-goo eyes.

"Stars. Was someone in the kitchen reporting our every move?" I muttered.

Peyton laughed. "Welcome back to Winterspell! Hot gossip like that doesn't stay under wraps for long."

"What's he like?" Tonya asked. "Does he smell as good as he looks?"

I held up a hand. "It *wasn't* a date."

"Mmhmm."

Linda swooped in to save me. "Come on, ladies. Let's give her some space. We don't want to scare her off." She glanced at her watch. "Besides, we need to get a move on if we want to log our miles and still have time for coffee."

Reluctantly, the other three agreed, and we set off. Peyton—thankfully—left the topic of Orion alone and we moved on to discussing other things. At one point, I got a side stitch and she pulled off to the side while I waited it out.

"Guess I pushed myself a little too hard, there," I said, grimacing at the pain radiating up my left side. The bruises and stiffness from my accident were starting to fade, and I'd likely overdone it, exhilarated to feel closer to normal again.

"It happens," Peyton said, jogging in place to keep warm. "I've actually considered hiring a coach. There's this guy some of the ladies work with. He mainly does marathon training, but I figure, if he can do that, he can probably help with the basic conditioning stuff, too."

"It's not a bad idea," I said, bending to the opposite side to stretch it out. The pain died down after a few minutes and we took off at a slower pace.

We finished our lap and met the others at the starting point. I rode with Peyton and Tonya while Claudette joined Linda in her car. We drove into town and got to Dragon's Gold right when they opened for the day. Peyton paid for my coffee, insisting it was her way of making up for the slight razzing she'd given me about Orion. We took a four-top table and added a chair so we could all sit together. The conversation was light and easy, and the coffee was rich and strong. The perfect combination.

Linda was the first to leave, with Claudette hot on her heels. By six thirty, we'd all gone our separate ways, promising to meet again the following morning. Tonya offered me a ride home, but I declined. Dragon's Gold wasn't all that far from my parents' house, and I had the last half a cup of my second refill to keep me warm.

After a shower and a fresh change of clothes, I took my laptop to the kitchen table and pulled up my travel blog. Something about the conversation with Orion last night had sparked my travel bug. With Jasmine's words of encouragement in my ears, I combed through my most recent article, about a trip to Seattle, and finally mustered up the courage to hit publish.

THE WINTERSPELL GAZETTE building was a small commercial space, with a brick facade and an old industrial feel with ironwork on the front doors and the interior. It was a hat tip to the old-school printing press, even though the paper was now run using every modern convenience and technology. I approached the front desk, where an elderly woman sat hunched over a crossword puzzle. Clearing my throat, she glanced up, her eyes bright. "Oh, I'm sorry. I didn't hear you come up." Her eyes went wide when she realized who I was. "Rosella Midnight! I'd heard you were back in town."

I was getting tired of this conversation.

"Yes, I am." I forced a polite smile. "I was wondering if you have an archive. I was hoping to go through the older issues, you know, catch up on what I've missed, and all that."

If she thought the request odd, she didn't comment. Instead, she bustled around the small desk and led me into a room with two glass doors. It was almost a smaller version of the records office, with rows and rows of filing cabinets. In the center of the room there was a podium with a wand sitting to one side, a faint tether of magic leading from the wand to the podium, almost like those chained pens in bank branches.

"Here you are," the receptionist said, showing me to the podium. "Since you have magic, all you have to do is feed a little of it through this wand, state the date of the issue, or certain story, and the papers will appear here in a neat stack, easy as you please."

"Nice. That's a nifty little piece of spellwork."

"I believe it was one of your grandmother's inventions," the woman said, with a quick smile up at me.

I almost laughed. Of course it was.

She left me alone in the room, closing the doors behind her, and I picked up the wand. Using the keywords *missing joggers*, drawers of the cabinets opened and a stack of papers flew toward me, compiling themselves neatly in front of me, just as the woman had promised.

I took the stack to one of the two tables and settled in. The top of the stack were the most recent issues, and I temporarily set those aside, having already gone through them after finding them in the Sugar Shack recycling pile. What I wanted were the older editions. Starting with the first reporting, right after Olivia's kidnapping, I combed through the information, typing notes into my phone as I went. I still wasn't sure what I was looking for, so I just wrote down any thought that popped into my head. Questions to ask. People to follow up with. Trying desperately to identify some kind of common thread.

Then it hit me.

Nearly launching out of my seat, I dug back through the papers I'd already set aside to confirm my suspicion. Sure enough, there it was, the answer staring back at me in black and white.

The woman at the desk hadn't told me what to do to send the papers back to their places, so I left them on the table, typed one more frantic note to myself, and then all but bolted from the office.

Outside, I paused on the sidewalk and pulled up my contacts list. Peyton had given me her number before leaving the coffee shop, and I dialed it. She answered on the third ring and I tried to steady my voice, even as a breathless tension built in my chest. "Peyton, hey, it's Rosella. Would you happen to have a number for that running coach you mentioned?"

AT FOUR O'CLOCK THAT AFTERNOON, I sat behind the wheel of my dad's truck. He'd gotten it running again the night before, after another session spent in the garage tinkering alongside Jake—whom I avoided like the plague. Dad agreed to let me borrow the old girl when I told him I had an appointment. He didn't ask what kind. Maybe he assumed it was some kind of "female" thing and thought better than to ask.

The house on the other side of the street belonged to a Rick Shaker, a personal trainer and running coach. I'd called him and we'd made an appointment for that evening at his in-home gym, so he could assess my form and set up a training program for me to follow.

Right at the top of the hour, I rang the doorbell on the side door leading into the garage, which, Rick had explained over the phone, doubled as his training space. A tall, fit man in his forties opened the door, offering a wide smile and an outstretched hand. "You must be Rosella Midnight."

"That's me," I said, taking his hand for a quick shake.

"It's nice to meet you," he said, taking a step back. Ushering me into the garage, he closed the door behind me. "Punctuality, too. I like that. Means you have a good training ethic."

I smiled as I took in the studio. All manner of workout equipment dominated the three-car converted garage. A variety of treadmills, weight machines, rows of dumbbells, resistance bands, and some tape marking different things on the padded floor. "Impressive studio you've got here. Do you do personal training in addition to coaching runners?"

"I do," Rick replied, coming to stand beside me, surveying his kingdom like a proud lion. "I'm a jack of all trades in the fitness world. Used to dabble in physique competitions years ago. But the training side has kind of taken over. You're lucky I had a space open this afternoon. Guess it was meant to be!"

He chuckled as he crossed the room to where a corner had been set aside for office space. An L-shaped desk hugged one wall, with a large computer monitor, and a whiteboard calendar hanging above.

"How did you hear about me anyway?" he asked, coming back toward me with a clipboard he'd snagged from the desk. "This is just a little paperwork to get us started. Waivers and health info."

I took the clipboard and pretended to write in my name at the top. "I got your name and number from Peyton. I've recently joined the Winterspell Runners Club."

"Oh! Peyton. She's a great girl." Rick smiled.

"You know, I heard you trained all three of the women who've gone missing," I said, glancing up from the paperwork just in time to gauge his reaction. I'd expected some sense of shock or shiftiness, but instead, he looked crestfallen.

"Olivia, Amber, and Krystal were all dedicated clients," he said, his tone matching his somber expression. "All three were interested in participating in next spring's Winterspell Marathon."

"I saw you, in the papers, posing with them at a charity run last year," I added.

"Yes," Rick replied with a slight nod. "The paper called and told me they were running those photos. I think someone with the charity must have given them to the editor. They said they wanted to show the women and their interests, passions, I guess. To make them more than just names in a headline."

"And what do you think happened to them?"

That's when Rick caught on. His head snapped up,

his eyes wide. "What do you mean? It was in the paper ... all about this, uh, serpent thing."

"You don't think it's weird that a sea serpent is only out to eat active women in their early-to-mid-thirties? You don't think it's odd that there haven't been any reports of missing pets or children, or other types of people?"

Rick took a slight step back. "I—I guess I never thought about it. The sheriff said it was more of an opportunity thing, you know, because they were always down by the lake, running at all hours, sometimes alone."

"And you would know their training schedules better than anyone, wouldn't you?"

"Wait—" He held up a hand. "You think *I* had something to do with Olivia, Amber, and Krystal's disappearances?"

"Did you?"

"No! Of—of course not!" He scoffed, shaking his head in disbelief. "Why would I want to hurt them?"

"I don't know, but you're the one thing they all had in common. You would have known their schedules, their habits, and I'm sure none of them would have thought twice about meeting you in a secluded area for a training session. You had the perfect opportunity with all three of them! And because you have a good reputation and probably went to the funerals and paid your respects, no one would have ever thought twice about you."

Rick backed up, holding out one hand, as though protecting himself. "You—you're crazy!"

His face had gone white as a sheet. A shiver of doubt ran through me for the first time since seeing his face in three of the newspaper clippings, posed with each of the missing women.

I'd been so sure … but now …

Had I misjudged it?

"How can I prove it to you? I didn't touch them—well, I mean, sometimes to help with a stretch or something, but … but never to try anything inappropriate and certainly not to hurt them or scare them!"

"Do you have alibis for the dates each of them went missing?" I asked.

Rick scurried back to the desk and snatched a black folio from atop a stack of magazines. "Here," he said, extending it to me, "I keep all of my appointments in there. You can check the days they went missing and call my clients. I see clients at the gym most of the day, and do trail runs and training here at home in the evenings. You'll see. It's all accounted for."

The book was filled with appointments and notes, some even scrawled in the margins because there wasn't enough space on the allotted dates. Rick Shaker was a busy man—especially in a small town. The logs couldn't all be real, could they? Maybe he'd filled it out, after the fact, to cover for himself?

"I'd rather you not call all of my clients and tell them you think I'm some kind of sick freak," Rick said, his voice steadying. "Maybe you could say you're a prospective client, and just want a testimonial, or something?"

I lifted a brow. "Tell you what, I'll just hand this over to Sheriff Templeton and let him and his detective decide what to do."

Rick Shaker didn't need to know I was on the sheriff's bad side.

"Please," Rick said, his eyes pleading. "This business is my entire life. There has to be some other way I can prove it to you. I didn't hurt any of those women; they were more than clients, they were friends."

"Well, maybe you wanted to be more than friends, and they didn't share those feelings."

Rick swore. "I'm a happily engaged man. I didn't—I don't—" He broke off; his expression changed, suddenly stony. "I think I should call a lawyer."

"I don't have the power to arrest you," I told him.

"No, but if you go poking around, harassing my clients, spreading these crackpot theories and lies, I'll have him sue you for slander!"

The joke would be on him, given the sorry state my bank account was in. But then, I supposed it was possible he could drag things out in court and I'd get up to my eyeballs in debt to a defense attorney. My parents would insist on helping … and I couldn't let that happen.

I flipped through the pages, each crammed full of appointments and bookings, save a weekend here or there marked as vacation. It would have taken a lot of work to go through and create something so detailed and precise on the off chance someone would come looking for it. Then there'd been the horrified look in his eyes at the mere suggestion he'd hurt the women. That also would have been hard to fake.

Shoving the book back at him, I relented. "Fine. Let's say I believe you. According to you, they were all clients and friends, so who do you think did this? You must have some theory beyond this ridiculous notion of a sea serpent. What else did they have in common?"

Rick's face fell, the momentary anger and outrage once again slipping into despair. "I wish I knew. Believe me, if there was anything I could do to bring the real monster to justice, I would."

The last spark of hope—the one that had all but flown me out of the newspaper office—died.

CHAPTER FOURTEEN

J left Rick's house and drove around in a foggy haze. Frustration and helplessness and old memories all swirled and swooped together, stitching my every muscle and nerve until my entire body felt like a trip wire. It took every ounce of resolve to keep from hitting the gas and peeling over the bridge, back into the non-magic world. Though, a part of me was starting to wonder if I belonged there either.

In Winterspell, there was one place guaranteed to take the edge off, and I found myself pulling into the parking lot of Merlin's Well, the town tavern. I cut the engine on the truck with a rough twist of my wrist and jammed the key ring into the pocket of my coat. Hoisting my purse on my shoulder, I jumped out the driver's side door and slammed it closed behind me. As I stalked to the door, a pair of guys in their thirties hurried to open the door for me.

I marched right up to the bar, slammed my purse down, and dropped onto one of the worn, wooden stools. The barkeep, a heavyset man with dark hair and a Scottish accent approached with a no-nonsense greeting. "What'll ya have, lass?"

"Whiskey, rocks. Make it a double."

The man gave me an approving glance, then went to get me the drink. It didn't slip my notice that he pulled down some of the good stuff from the second to the top row of the myriad of bottles lining the back wall. He poured the drink with neat efficiency and placed it in front of me. "You just let me know if ya need another."

"Cheers," I said, raising my glass to no one in particular.

The barkeep smiled and scuttled off to speak with the two men who'd held the door for me.

Merlin's Well hadn't changed a thing since my last visit, a good five years ago. After Grandpa Rodgers's funeral, half the town had shown up to salute the man. I'd gone home with Jake that night, craving comfort and a distraction. In the end, all I'd managed to do was dredge up fresh heartbreak for both of us when I left the following Monday morning at first light, eager to leave Winterspell behind once more.

I sipped the whiskey, savoring the burn.

The bar was well-loved and worn, like a pair of good shoes. Comfortable and broken-in. A little rough around the edges, but somehow, that only made it better. The salt and pepper shakers were always low, the ketchup bottles stingy, but the food was deep-fried and hot, and the drinks were strong and generous, so you put up with the uneven tables and the fact that not a single chair in the joint matched anymore.

Likewise, the barkeep, Gerry, was much the same. He'd never married. The bar was his wife. He had a small studio above the bar. I'd never been up there, but I imagined it looked about the same as the bar itself, a collection of knick-knacks and mismatched furniture and dishes, functional but not pretty.

As I considered the two men at the pool table—both of whom were paying more attention to a pretty brunette waiting on a table across the bar, than the game—someone sat down on the stool beside me. Turning, I locked onto a pair of storm-cloud gray eyes.

"I thought you said you came here on Friday nights," I said, smiling.

One corner of Jake's mouth quirked. "It's just been one of those days."

"Buy you a drink?" I asked, hoping Gerry would let me start a tab.

Jake nodded. "Okay."

Gerry came over, a wary look in his eye as he spotted the pair of us. "Now, this here is a real flashback," he said, pointing. "Be careful that you don't go breaking this young lady's heart, driving her out of town again."

I blinked. Was that the rumor around town?

"I promise," Jake said, holding up a hand, palm out like he was taking a solemn oath. "I'll do no such thing."

Gerry threw me a wink. "Good to hear. Now, what can I get to quench yer thirst?"

Jake ordered an ale Gerry kept on tap, and the barkeep went to retrieve it. Once Jake had the drink, I twisted on my seat to face him. "People think you broke my heart and *that's* why I left?"

"That's what *some* people think," he replied. "I've never taken an official survey. The people who know us, know the truth."

The truth. The messy, dragged-out, painful truth.

"I'm still sorry about that," I said.

"El, please, let's not. I meant what I said the other day: it's in the past, let's leave it there."

I sipped at my whiskey, not as eager for the burn as when I'd walked into the tavern. Jake drank a little, then spun around and considered the rest of the room, his elbows propped casually behind him on the bar as he leaned back. "Good news from the insurance company," he said, glancing at me. "I'm still waiting on a few parts to come in, but I should have your car back to you by the middle of next week."

"Yeah. Assuming I can come up with my deductible," I mumbled.

Jake lifted a brow. "Didn't you have some fancy newspaper job in the big city?"

I couldn't help but laugh softly. "Yeah, turns out, that doesn't pay as well as one would think, especially when it requires living in one of the country's most expensive cities." I frowned, debating just how much to share. It was an odd feeling. Jake and I shared everything for such a huge chunk of my life, that it was strange to try and filter things out of a story.

"That's why you're back here?" Jake asked.

"I'm just figuring things out. I'll find the money for the deductible."

Jake nodded slowly. The gears in his mind were working. "Well, if you need, I could—"

"Jake … no. I can't let you do that. You're already helping me a lot, dealing with the paperwork and all that stuff. I'm working at Sugar Shack. I'll ask my dad if I can get a draw on my paycheck."

Of course, that would mean coming clean to my family about my dismal finances.

"All right, but if you need help, just—"

"Thank you, Jake."

Twisting, he grabbed his glass of ale. He smiled at me before he took a drink. "Who would have thought we'd be here, sharing a drink like this?"

I laughed. "Not me."

He chuckled. "No, I guess not."

"You want to talk about your crappy day?" I asked, hoping to shrink out of the spotlight.

He laughed. "Not really. I'd just bore you. Work stuff, and all that."

We nursed our drinks, listening to the chatter of the

other patrons and the music filtering from the ancient jukebox in one corner of the room.

"Word on the street is you and Sheriff Templeton got into it in the town square," Jake said, giving a half-cocked grin. "You haven't lost your knack for making friends."

I rolled my eyes. "Yeah, I'm surprised he didn't bring backup, you know, in case I decided to take over a flock of birds and go all Alfred Hitchcock on the town."

Jake laughed. "Oh, come on, El. You know not everyone thinks like that around here."

I shook my head, giving him a bemused smile. "You always see the best in people, don't you?"

He shrugged. "I try."

My smile turned wistful and I threw back the rest of my whiskey, quickly flagging Gerry for a refill. "You're a good man, Jake March."

He glanced at my empty glass. "How many of those did you have before I got here?" he teased.

I shoved his shoulder playfully. "Come on, I can't compliment you?"

We laughed and Gerry gave us a wide grin when he came back over with the whiskey bottle.

We were a few sips into our second round when the jukebox changed and a familiar song filtered in through the speakers over the bar. A rush surged through me as my brain picked up the first few chords. Jake noticed, too. We glanced at each other, then smiled even wider, realizing we were thinking the same thing.

Jake slid from the stool and set his glass on the bar. Jerking his chin toward the jukebox, he grinned. "For old times' sake?"

I hesitated for a second, but his easy smile was impossible to resist. I set my whiskey glass on the bar beside his drink, and we shed our winter coats before taking to the makeshift dance floor. The eight-by-eight patch of linoleum in front of the jukebox, where the longtime lovebirds, the one-night standers, and everyone in between could get their groove on.

Jake and I fell somewhere in the middle. Longtime lovebirds, but that felt like another lifetime ago, though as soon as he placed a hand on my back and took my other hand, it was like those years melted away. Memories of high school homecoming, starlit slow dances in the middle of nowhere, and the painful dance lessons we'd been needled into taking after his mother bought us lessons for Christmas.

Jake smiled. "Looks like we still remember some of the steps."

I giggled. "You were thinking about that, too?"

"How could I forget?" He grinned. "I had to ice my toes for a week afterward!"

I rolled my eyes, but couldn't help laughing.

"My mom should have bought us lessons to stomp grapes into wine," he teased. "You would have been aces at that."

Laughing together, he swung me out and I spun, my muscles relaxing. It felt so good to laugh, especially in the aftermath of such a craptastic day. "Well, at least I did my *stomping* on the right rhythm," I fired back with a grin as he tugged me back close. "You couldn't hit the beat if you had a big rubber mallet and bullseye marking the spot."

Jake's brows lifted as he barked out a laugh. "Oh, is that so?"

He dropped my hands and took a step back, showing off some choreographed moves. They didn't fit the song, but he hit the moves cleanly and didn't look half bad. Oh, who was I kidding … he looked great. Better than before—a fact I would only begrudgingly admit to myself and would never share with anyone else, least of all Grandma Rose. What was it she'd said? Aging like a fine wine.

I had to agree.

Jake did a spin, then ended with a pose as though tipping the brim of an invisible cowboy hat, flashing a wink, before he took a little theater bow.

Clapping, I laughed. "Okay, okay, it looks like you may have done a little practicing since then," I admitted, smiling as he took me back in his arms.

"Kaylee got married last fall," he said. "She made us all take dance lessons for this big, goofy number at the end. Something she saw on YouTube, I guess."

"Aha. What else you got?"

He spun me around again and moved up behind

me, his hands on my waist. Butterflies exploded into glittering fireworks and I had to stop myself from closing my eyes and getting carried away by the way it felt to have him so close. The music changed and he spun me back around to face him, our eyes wide with surprise.

Jake dropped my hand and took a step back, his chest rising and falling a little too quickly. "This was probably a bad idea."

"Jake—"

He left the floor and went back to the bar. People were watching us with curiosity, and my cheeks warmed. "Jake!"

He tugged his wallet free, dropped a twenty on the bar, and signaled for Gerry. "Thanks, man. See you Friday for the darts tournament." Grabbing his coat, he headed for the door.

Gerry glanced at me, then ping-ponged back to Jake's retreating form. "See you Friday, laddie."

I watched him go, then looked down at the money. "Gerry, can I start a tab? I can pay next week."

Gerry waved me off. "That was a welcome home drink, Rosella. On me."

The sweet, simple gesture brought tears to my eyes and I hurried from the bar, called a *thank you* over my shoulder as I went.

Jake was still in the parking lot, behind the wheel of his truck. He'd only had the one beer, but I would have bet anything he was sitting there, debating whether or not he should wait a little longer before driving off. He saw me and made up his mind. He started the engine.

"Jake! Please—"

He rolled down the driver's window. "Ella, please, I can't do this again. *We* can't go there again. We both know where it ends. It will be just like after your grandfather's funeral. We'll have one night, and I'll start thinking maybe it will be different this time, and then, just like that—*boom*—you're gone again come morning. I can't, El."

The raw emotion in his voice broke something inside me and the tears that had formed at the corners of my eyes slipped free.

"I'm sorry," I said, scrubbing the palm of my hand across my cheeks. Sniffling, I nodded. "You're right. It's just been a crappy day and I—"

I stopped short of calling him a distraction. That would only hurt him more. And there was a part of me that knew it wasn't true. At least, not entirely.

"I'll see you around," I said.

Jake stared at me, his face a mixture of emotions. His jaw went tense and he inclined his head. "Next week. For the car. I'll call you."

"Right!" I breathed a ragged laugh. "Thanks. Next week."

Before I could melt down into a full-on puddle, I hurried two spaces down and climbed in behind the wheel of my dad's beat-up truck. I dug the keys from my pocket and jammed them into the ignition. I turned them, and nothing happened.

"No," I groaned. "No, no, no. Not now. Please!"

Twisting again, I silently sent a plea to Mother Nature herself.

Nothing. Not even a sputter.

"You're not even trying!" I growled at the truck, as though it could hear me.

A tapping on my window startled me, and I glanced up, wide-eyed, to see Jake standing on the other side. With a sigh of resignation, I pulled the keys from the ignition and slid out of the truck's cab.

Jake flashed a rueful smile. "This truck will be the death of me."

"Seriously," I groaned. "Can we push it into the lake or something? Then my dad would have to buy another one."

Jake chuckled as he went around to the front and lifted the hood. "Problem is, your dad is one of my main customers, and he tips well. So ..."

I laughed softly and joined him, though I had no idea what any of the various parts and gears even did. My mechanic skills ended at changing a flat tire and swapping out windshield wipers—they tended to take a beating in Portland.

Jake poked around for a minute while I stood beside him and braced against the cold. Night had fallen, and while it wasn't snowing, it certainly felt cold enough for it. "I'll have to get it back to my shop," Jake said. "I'll come tow it in the morning."

He shut the hood and gestured for me to follow him. "Come on, I'll give you a ride home."

Right. Cause that won't be awkward.

"I can call Matty or Jasmine," I said, already digging into my purse for my phone. "You go on ahead. I'll be fine."

Jake stepped closer and lowered the phone gently. My eyes lifted, meeting his. "I'd like to try and be your friend, El. Do you think we could do that? This is a small town, and we can't be ducking and dodging each other at every turn." He paused and drew in a breath. "I got carried away in there. Old memories, and all that. Please, just let me take you home. I'm not going to leave you out here freezing in a parking lot."

Sighing, I put my phone away and followed Jake to his truck. He pulled open the passenger door and I climbed in. Our eyes met through the glass when he closed it, holding the contact for a long moment, before hurrying around the front and climbing back behind the wheel.

Thankfully, Merlin's Well was only a ten-minute drive from my parents' house, though the pained silence made it seem longer. Jake pulled into the driveway and I hesitated. Should I say something? And if so, what?

"Thanks for the drink," I told him, though techni-cally Gerry had given it to me.

Jake nodded. "Sure thing."

"Um, good luck on Friday."

He turned to me, his brows quizzical.

"At the, uh, dart thing?"

"Oh! Right. Yeah … thanks. I'm pretty terrible, but I buy the first round, so they let me hang around." He chuckled, though the warmth in the low rumble of his voice never reached his eyes. "I'll call next week. About the car."

"Thanks. Again, I appreciate it. And the ride. I'll tell my dad about the truck."

Jake laughed softly. "I wouldn't mention the push-it-into-the-lake plan. He's sensitive about the old girl."

I smiled, then slid out of the truck and hurried up to the front porch. Jake waited until I went inside to back out and drive away. Sighing, I watched him drive away through the skylight on the right side of the front door, before letting the sheer curtain fall back into place, blocking out the frigid night.

CHAPTER FIFTEEN

"That's the second time I've seen you with Jake March in one week," Grandma Rose commented, as I padded into the living room a moment later.

"Third, if you count your *hilarious* little setup on the night I got here," I said, sinking into the armchair.

Grandma Rose grinned; clearly she had no regrets. After a moment of silent gloating, she sobered, her wise eyes growing wistful. "First loves are hard to fall out of, and impossible to forget, Ella."

"I don't know that I want to forget Jake, but I do wish my heart would stop doing this weird twisty, stabby thing every time I see him."

Grandma Rose chuckled softly. "You know I loved your grandfather, with every ounce of my heart, but he wasn't my first love."

My brows lifted. "He wasn't?"

It was hard to imagine Grandma Rose with anyone other than my Grandpa Rodger. Rose and Rodger, they'd been like peanut butter and jelly, a classic, timeless combination.

"His name was Vernon," Grandma Rose continued, her voice quiet as her eyes grew wistful. "We were neighbors growing up. He used to come help my father with work around the farm. See, after the wizard's war, my father wasn't able to keep up with the place all on his own. So, Vernon came and helped. He was older than me by three years, but things like that don't matter. He used to work all day on the farm, and then we'd spend hours wandering the woods at the back acreage of my parents' property. We'd talk about life. Books we'd read, or we'd make up stories to make each other laugh."

"What was he like?" I asked.

"He was smart as a whip, handsome as the day is long, and could always cheer me up, even on the darkest of days."

"He sounds pretty great," I said, then smiled. "Although, I'm really glad you chose Grandpa. He was the best."

Grandma Rose's eyes grew wistful, a slight sheen to her blue irises. "That he was. One of a kind."

"What happened to Vernon?" I asked. "Why didn't you two end up together?"

"Well, my dear girl, it was a little something like what you and Jake went through. He wanted to take that sharp mind of his and make something of himself, something bigger than what he could find in our small farm town. He asked me to go with him, to marry him even, but I had to turn him down. That wasn't the right path for me."

"Oh." I glanced down at my hands. There were questions I wanted to ask her, but didn't know how without revealing the truth.

After a moment, I looked up at her. "Grandma, there was someone else," I said softly. "In Portland. I was—I was engaged, to a brilliant photographer named Leo."

Grandma Rose nodded, as though she already knew. "Jasmine told me."

My eyes widened.

"Now, don't be upset with her," Grandma Rose interjected before I could land on an emotion. "She was worried about you. We all were. You stopped coming home to visit, calls were infrequent and often short when we did manage to reach you. We thought you were maybe falling into a depression, and wanted to go down and check on you, but Jasmine stepped in and told us about the young man, and explained you wanted to keep it a secret, and that you wouldn't appreciate us barging into your new life."

My heart sank. I hated that they felt like they had to stay away. I'd wanted out of Winterspell, not my own family, despite our differences. "I'm sorry I didn't tell you."

Grandma Rose chuckled. "Oh, dear girl, you're entitled to your privacy. I do wish I could have met him. Jasmine said he was quite a piece of eye candy."

I laughed so hard I snorted. "Oh, Grandma. We need to get you a boyfriend."

"Nah. I like the ones in my books better than any of the old toads shuffling around this town."

"Book boyfriends are always better than real life ones," I concurred.

"Book boyfriends?" Grandma Rose repeated, a quirked grin on her thinning lips. "I quite like that!"

"Jake says he wants to try and be friends," I told her after a moment. "Do you think that's even possible? Without crossing the lines? Could you and Vernon have ever been just friends?"

Grandma considered the question thoughtfully, then dipped her chin. "Perhaps," she said, "though, I think it's difficult with one's first love. There's something about it that gets into the bloodstream."

"So, what should I do? Just duck behind my shopping cart if I run into him at the grocery store or jump into the lake if I see him on the opposite side of the road?"

"I can't answer that for you, Ella. I think you'll have to decide if Jake's friendship is worth the pain of having to keep your heart in check."

Standing, she shuffled closer and patted me on the back of the hand. "You'll find your way, dear girl. I've never doubted that."

"Thank you, Grandma. That means a lot to me."

She smiled as she turned away. "Now, if you'll excuse me, I have a date with one of my book boyfriends."

Tossing me a wink, she headed down the hall in search of her weathered paperback.

AFTER WARMING up a serving of my mom's veggie lasagna for dinner, I went out to the barn in search of Karma. "Don't tell me you're turning feral again," I said, lighting a lantern as I wandered inside. "Karma?"

My magic could sense the various creatures in the barn. The hens, safely tucked in for the night; Tumnus, up in the rafters, likely readying for a night flight; and a few small rodents. Apparently, Flotsam and Jetsam's mouse-hunting lessons weren't going all that well. With no sign of the three cats I started to get a little worried. Karma had been rescued off the street, but she was young and I'd always taken care of her from afar.

Where were they? If Flotsam and Jetsam led her into harm's way …

"Ah, good evening, Rosella," a hooty voice called overhead.

Glancing up, I saw Tumnus, perched on a wooden beam. "Hi, Tumnus. Have you seen the cats? There's a little black one, goes by the name Karma. I'm afraid

Flotsam and Jetsam might be up to no good. You know how they can be."

Tumnus laughed, the sound a short series of trills. *"Oh, yes. They're out in your mother's toolshed. They all fell asleep in a little puddle, in a crate of empty feed sacks."*

Relief flooded my chest and I smiled. "Oh, good. Thank you. Are you getting ready to go out for the night?"

"I was considering it. It's awful cold out there tonight. I stuck a wing out to test it and—" He ruffled his feathers and screwed up his little oval face. *"Brrr! Perhaps I'd best stay here and keep you company."*

I smiled. "I'm not sure how good of company I'll be. It's kind of been one of those days."

Tumnus swooped down and landed on the railing of what had been built as a horse stable, back when Candice had her pony phase. Skipper, the old little pony she'd named after her favorite Barbie doll, had since passed into the Stardust Realm, and my parents never bought another horse. The property wasn't big enough for a full-sized horse, and they were busy enough that caring for another pony was too big a task.

"What's wrong, Rosella? You look sad."

"I am sad," I replied, sinking down onto two stacked hay bales, using them as a makeshift chair.

"Is this about those missing women?"

I nodded and caught him up on everything that had happened since I'd originally asked for his help. Tumnus was a great listener and absorbed my words in attentive silence. Having spent most of his life around humans he was far more interested in our comings and goings than wild animals would be.

"—and now, tomorrow afternoon, Valkyrie will be hunted and killed, and there's nothing more I can do to try and save her," I concluded.

"Take heart, Rosella. There is still time. And who knows, this hunter might not be able to find her! You did warn her to stay hidden. That lake is very deep."

Somehow, I doubted it. Orion's resume was impressive, and even if he didn't find her, the warden wouldn't easily call off the hunt and reopen the investigation, especially with nothing but my testimony. I needed a clue, a lead, some shred of evidence.

"I could go talk to the reporter," I said. "I meant to this morning, but I saw the link, with the running coach, and got too excited. Ugh! I should have waited and talked to the reporter first."

"Let's go out tonight," Tumnus said. *"We'll ask every creature we can find. I'll find the birds, you take the ground. There are rats, cats, dogs, gophers, moles, deer, ducks, geese! All manner of creatures who might have seen something."*

"Tumnus, we can't interview an entire town and forest's worth of animals in one night," I replied.

"Not if we don't try!"

He tilted his head in that strange owl-like manner, his black eyes glittering with determination. If Tumnus was willing to brave the cold to help, the least I could do would be to tag along. It was one heck of a Hail

Mary, but it probably beat sitting in my room, sinking in the dread—or worse, thinking about Jake and that dance.

Squeezing my eyes closed against the flickers of the memory, I pushed up from the hay bales. "All right. Let me go get thicker gloves on. Meet back here when the church bells strike one? I have to work tomorrow, early shift, and I'll need at least a few hours' sleep if I don't want to accidentally send my hand through the bread slicer."

Tumnus blinked. He likely had no idea what a bread slicer was.

He didn't stick around to ask; he spread his wings and sailed through the small opening in the side of the barn, flying off into the night.

I went inside, bundled up with another layer and the thickest gloves I could find in the mudroom storage bins. They were likely my father's, and a size too big for me, but they were thick and warm, and would keep me from giving up too early due to the cold.

I'd likely need every minute I could get.

CHAPTER SIXTEEN

*W*ithout a vehicle, I was forced to stay close to the town for the beginning of my search. Luckily, the weather had driven people home after the work day ended and the shops closed, leaving the streets deserted and quiet. It made it easier for my magic to reach out and find animals nearby when I could focus all of my attention on the task, allowing a wider net of magic.

My first interview was with a black-and-white cat found patrolling the alley behind the fish market. After getting his attention and explaining my mission, I showed him pictures of the three women I'd taken from the newspaper, and asked if he'd seen them. He said he hadn't and went back to picking through the leftovers in the dumpster. Next, I found a pigeon picking through the debris swept off the sidewalk in front of a small cafe, looking for crumbs. I'd brought a pocketful of snacks, in case I needed some extra encouragement. I offered the bird a small portion of granola and lured it closer as I explained my predicament.

The bird looked at the pictures, its beady eyes blinking rapidly as I shuffled through the three images, taken from my collection of news clippings. *"That one,"* he said, when I got to Krystal's.

"You know her? Do you know where she is?"

"She feeds the ducks at the park on her lunch breaks," the bird told me. *"I like to go after those quackers are done. She's nice. She doesn't chase me away like the others do."*

I sighed. It was a nice anecdote, but not helpful in learning anything about her disappearance. I thanked the bird, dropped another handful of treats, and continued on.

From there, it got harder. The weather had driven the local animals undercover, along with the human residents. I found a few more birds pecking around the street for scraps, but none of them had anything of interest to say.

A frosty fog rolled in as the night grew later. My cheeks were frozen, and the extra layer of clothing wasn't making it any more pleasant to be searching the streets. Giving up on the main strip through town, I went down along the water and started toward the apartment complex where Olivia had lived. Maybe there was a community of cats or squirrels that might have seen something leading up to her disappearance.

I figured I could go there, and it was the only one of the three I'd been able to find an address for. The paper had listed her as a resident of the building; the other two hadn't had any clues listed as to where they lived, and I doubted Sheriff Templeton or his detective would share the information with me. Orion might be able to get it. That would be a last, last resort.

Most of the wildlife steered clear of the town. It was a long shot any of them had seen anything. Looking to the tree line on the other side of the lake, I hoped Tumnus was having more luck than me.

As it turned out, there were a few cats living outside the apartment building. Someone had stacked some old tires at the back of the building, and I found two cats curled up inside, trying to stay warm. They sleepily answered my questions, but said they'd only moved into the makeshift nest a few weeks before, when they'd been scared off from the colony of feral cats living at the campgrounds on the other side of the lake. People at the apartment fed them and they had a relatively warm and dry place to sleep. Before leaving, I told them about my parents' barn and offered it up for when the snow started to fall.

I left the apartment building just as the church bells rang out at midnight. It would take a good thirty minutes to walk back to my parents' house. Besides that, I was freezing. I couldn't stay out much longer. I'd go back, talk to Tumnus, and then go to bed. I'd tried not to let myself get my hopes up, but my shoulders sagged as I trudged back through town.

Then, through the fog, tiny clacking footsteps sounded on the concrete. I glanced up and realized it was the sound of nails scratching against the sidewalk as a small white dog raced down the street. Squinting, I realized I knew the dog.

"Fluffy?"

The dog stopped, his ears perked.

I reached out with tendrils of magic, beckoning him closer. Dogs don't usually take much persuasion, as most of them are already trusting of humans. Fluffy— oddly enough—took a little effort. Eventually, I got him to come closer. I checked the tag on his collar just to be sure.

Fluffy was engraved in the bone-shaped silver tag, along with a phone number that I assumed belonged to Linda. "What are you doing out here, all alone?" I asked, ruffling the dog's fur.

"Can't go back there! Not to her! Must keep running!"

I blinked as the tiny dog's reply came to me, his eyes darting up and down the street. Was he looking for Linda?

"Fluffy, slow down, what's going on? What happened?"

The dog paused, blinking as he looked up at me. *"You can hear me?"*

Nodding, I asked him to elaborate.

"She's awful! Please, don't make me go back there!"

"Linda?" I asked. Glancing around, as though she, too, might emerge from the fog.

Fluffy spun around so fast, he would have given himself whiplash if not for his short little spine. *"Where?"* he shrieked.

Scooping the dog up, I carried him a few steps, ignoring his frantic protests. "I'm not going to hurt you!" I insisted, wrestling the squirming dog in my arms. "Fluffy, stop! I'm trying to help you! Tell me why you ran away. What did Linda do?"

"She's going to kill them! On the full moon!" the little dog yelped. *"And I won't stand by and watch it. It's too awful! She's lost her mind!"*

I stopped walking. A chill that had nothing to do with the weather surrounded me. *"Linda is the kidnapper?"*

"Yes, and she's got another one. The last one. Now ... she's going through with it. When she first started talking about it, I thought it was the ramblings of a woman mad with grief, but now—"

The little dog shuddered in my arms and I held him closer, picking my feet up again. My heart slammed into my chest. "What is she going to do?"

"It's a sacrifice. Some kind of blood magic. She's got all these old books and parchments ... she doesn't do anything but study them. Over and over and over again. She's obsessed!"

I glanced over my shoulder as I scurried down the

street, clutching the dog to my chest. "I'll take you home with me, but you have to tell me everything."

"Fine, fine, just don't call her!"

We got to my parents' house and I took Fluffy to the barn. Tumnus wasn't back yet, so we waited for him near the chickens' stall, warming up under the outer ring of the orange glow from the large heat-emitting lamp hanging overhead.

In the chicken coop, Merryweather stirred. Peering at me, she straightened her neck. *"Worms?"*

I slashed a hand through the air. *"Not now. Go back to sleep."*

Meanwhile, Fluffy followed his nose around the barn, likely on overload with all of the new smells and senses. When he circled back to me, he was ready to talk.

"Olivia was first," he began, panting excitedly between sentences. *"Linda called her one day, asked her to come over for lunch. Olivia didn't know what she was walking into. It was a trap. Linda cast some sort of binding spell on her and locked her in the spare bedroom ... it used to be my Ariana's bedroom."*

"Ariana? That's Linda's daughter? She mentioned she lost her some time ago."

"That's how I wound up stuck with her," Fluffy huffed. *"I thought she was going to stop. She got so upset after taking Olivia and I think she wanted to let her go, but then, she couldn't do that, could she? So, then she took Amber. They knew each other from the running club, too. Linda did the*

same thing. Asked her over to lunch, or tea, and did the same thing. Locked her up with Olivia. Again with Krystal. She keeps them fed and they have a bathroom to use, but the windows are sealed with some kind of spell. No one can hear them scream for help and they can't break out."

"What does she want with them? You said something about a ... sacrifice?"

I cringed. The word was so dark and ominous.

"She needed one more. Something about a full set for the full moon," Fluffy replied. *"That's why she invited Peyton over—"*

"Peyton?" I shot to my feet. "She took Peyton?"

"That's how I got away!" Fluffy yelped. *"She had her over for dinner tonight, but Peyton got a call and tried to leave early. She got to the driveway before Linda got her binding spell ready. And she left the door open. I ran past her. I ran down the street and found someone who left their garage cracked and I hid out until it got dark and they started to close it. And then you found me."*

Fluffy sat down, his fur fluffing out around him, a dramatic flourish to the end of his tale.

"A full set?" I repeated, something about it sticking out to me. "A full set of elemental powers! Air, wind, fire, and water. Peyton must be the last one. A fire witch."

Eying the dog, I frowned. "How do you know all of this?"

He was either the world's most observant dog, or Linda was a Chatty Cathy.

Apparently, it was the latter.

"She tells me everything!" Fluffy complained. *"What she eats, what she reads, where she's going, when she's going to bed. She thinks we're best friends! She takes me shopping with her and she even makes me follow her into the bathroom!"*

I blinked. "Wow. That's some stage-five clinger stuff right there."

"Tell me about it." The dog sighed. He looked around. *"This place is pretty nice. Can I stay here?"*

I smiled. Flotsam and Jetsam would have a thing— or twenty—to say about that idea. "Tell you what, I will find you the world's best home, but first, you have to help me get Olivia, Amber, Krystal, and Peyton to safety. Will you do that?"

The dog reared back. *"How are we supposed to do that?"*

"I have an idea." I rose from the hay bale pile. "I just need to make a phone call."

"THE DOG TOLD YOU ALL THIS?" Orion asked, his voice still thick from sleep when he'd answered my call.

"Yes," I said impatiently. "We have two nights until the full moon, but we can't let them sit there another night. Can you call in someone from the agency? You know, a real, kick-in-the-door type?"

Rustling noises filtered through the phone. "Where are you?"

"At my parents' house, in the barn. Everyone is asleep."

"Right." More background noise. "I'll be there in ten. Don't move."

"Okay." I bobbed my head, glancing down at Fluffy, who'd crashed out in a pile of loose straw, exhausted from his mad dash. "But please hurry."

Orion grunted a reply and hung up the phone.

"Wow," I said to myself, slipping the phone back into my coat pocket. "Someone sure needs his beauty sleep."

True to his word, Orion's truck rumbled up the drive ten minutes later. I stirred Fluffy, apologizing for waking him, and hurried out to the driveway. The last thing I needed was my family peeping out the window and seeing me speeding off in the middle of the night with the town's new heartthrob.

"Let's go," I said breathlessly, buckling up. I held Fluffy on my lap. "He's going to lead us there."

Fluffy gave a sharp bark.

Orion cringed. "Right."

Linda lived in a gated neighborhood on the outskirts of town, where the properties had large, well-manicured lots and plenty of space between the homes. The street was lined with mature trees. Their branches were empty now, but I knew the area, and come spring, they would sprout pretty pink petals before turning a rich purple color in the summer.

All of the homes were dark inside, with only porch lanterns and street lamps giving any light. All except for one. I knew it was Linda's before Fluffy could identify it. The two-story craftsman was lit up like a Christmas tree, and I imagined Linda inside, frantically trying to find her lost dog.

Fluffy confirmed it, quivering a little as Orion pulled alongside the curb on the opposite side of the street and put the truck into park. *"That's it,"* he said, ducking out of sight.

"Crap," I said. "I was hoping she'd be asleep. This is going to be tricky."

"The agency said they'll send someone out tomorrow to investigate," Orion said.

Horror-stricken, I turned to him. *"Tomorrow?"*

"Rosella, it's one in the morning," he said gently. "They'll need a search warrant, which requires permission from a council member, and council members do not appreciate being woken up in the middle of the night. Trust me, it's best they wait until morning, when the council member will be in more of a mood to listen. We're working with paper-thin evidence here."

I blinked. The words felt like a sting. "I literally have an eyewitness to all three—now four—kidnappings!"

Orion held up a hand. "I believe you, but will the council take your word for it?"

"They know all about my power," I replied harshly. "Why would I make this up?"

"I'm not arguing, I'm just playing devil's advocate. Trust me, I've worked inside councils' red tape maze most of my adult life. It's not cut and dried."

"Forget this," I said, digging out my phone. "I didn't want to have to do this, because I know I'm not his favorite person right now, but I'm calling Sheriff Templeton. Someone needs to get out here, now!"

Orion stilled my hand. I looked up and met his dark eyes; they looked black in the low lighting. "You're sure they're in there?"

"I'd bet my life on it."

He took a beat, then exhaled and threw open his door. "Then, let's go."

CHAPTER SEVENTEEN

"Come on!"

Orion darted across the street, sticking to the shadows between the soft rings of light pooling under the street lamps. Fluffy growled at me when I started to pick him up. *"I'm not going back in there!"* he snapped, baring his tiny teeth.

Sighing, I didn't bother trying to convince him that I wouldn't let Linda keep him. "Okay, stay here. I might need your help before this is all over." I started to close the door, then remembered something and leaned back in. "Where is she keeping the women?"

Fluffy trembled. *"There's a daylight basement. They're down there, in the guest suite."*

"Got it. Thanks, Fluffy."

Shutting the door carefully, I turned and cut across the street, following the same path Orion had taken. He was waiting for me at the edge of the property, tucked behind a tree trunk. "They're in the basement," I whispered, gesturing around the side of the house where a stepping stone path led to a wooden gate. "Let's go around back and see if we can get inside. Fluffy told me there's a window in the room she's keeping them in, but it's got some kind of spell on it, making the room soundproof along with keeping them locked in."

Orion nodded. He didn't seem concerned. That's when it hit me that I still had no idea what kind of magic he possessed. I'd seen him light a ball of flames, so he had at least some fire magic. He was good at tracking, but even humans could be excellent trackers. Did his magic help with his work? Or was that more a natural inclination?

There wasn't time to ask now. Orion streaked toward the gate and I followed. The fence was a few inches taller than Orion, and he had to be over six feet. He tried the gate, and frowned. It looked like an ordinary garden gate, but the latch refused to move. "It's got some kind of security spell," he explained, trying it once more. "Step back."

He spread his arms, bumping me back a few small steps. Closing his eyes, he whispered something under his breath, and a ball of blue flame appeared in his right palm. It burned almost white-hot but didn't scorch his skin. It was the sign of a fire mage, a level—or more— above a normally gifted fire wielder.

Orion guided the flame to the gate and the metal latch fell to the grass, the fire cutting through the enchanted metal like a hot knife into a stick of butter. Then, just as quickly as he'd called it forth, the flames vanished.

He opened the gate, moving slowly, in case there were other security measures waiting for us on the other side. The stepping stone path led down a slight slope and I realized how massive the house must be. What I'd thought were two levels were actually three, with the full daylight basement hidden from the street view. Whatever Linda did for work, it clearly paid well. The backyard was not as manicured as the front, but still didn't look too bad. It was a lot of property to maintain. She likely had groundskeepers come and tackle the front, but hadn't wanted them poking around the back, where the basement was on full display.

The lights in the basement weren't on, the entire bank of windows and the double glass doors still dark. Had she already searched the basement for Fluffy? Or was something else going on upstairs? A shiver crept up my spine. Fluffy said we had until the full moon, in two days' time, but there was something foreboding about the house that made me wonder if Linda wasn't in there changing her plans.

I placed a hand on Orion's back and he turned toward me. "What's the plan?" I asked.

He studied the darkened windows. "If they're being kept down here, we need to find which room. Maybe I can break the spell and we can get them out of here tonight."

He closed his eyes as he muttered a spell in a language I did not know. When he stopped speaking, he waited. Listening. Suddenly, his eyes popped back open, intense and stormy. He illuminated another ball of flame and began using it to cut through the three sides of the glass. The fire was so precise. I'd never seen a fire mage do such skilled, detailed work. Normally fire mages like to show off their power with big fire-balls or other pyrotechnic-styled displays. It was clear Orion was on a different skill level, able to hone the flame with such control. Fire was a dangerous element, it wanted to be wild, to spread and grow, so to be able to whittle it down showed the true level of a practi-tioner's skill.

"I have an idea," he said, pulling the flame back before making the final cut along the top. He pulled a roll of duct tape from his Batman-style utility belt, created two loops with the sticky side facing out, and attached them to the nearly severed pane. "Hold onto these, think of them as handles."

I slipped my fingers through the makeshift loops he'd made with the tape, seeing his plan. As he cut the top of the window, the glass would crash to the ground and shatter. If his idea worked, I'd be able to keep that from happening, with the loops of strong tape hope-fully keeping it from falling at all.

Holding my breath, I gripped the loops as he made the final cut. The glass sagged but the tape held. Orion grabbed the top and carefully pulled it from the window, setting the large sheet of cut glass on the ground, leaned up against the house. He tossed an orb of light into the room and boosted me up and over, whispering for me to be careful not to slice myself on the cut glass. He followed, moving like a graceful cat. Or maybe a cat burglar. Something told me this wasn't his first time breaking into a locked building. That would have to be a question for another day. At the moment, I was just grateful not to be alone, and to have made it inside Linda's house on silent feet.

The room we entered appeared to be an office, but instead of filing cabinets and a bookcase, there were two long tables on opposite sides of the room, both of them covered in a myriad of papers, parchments, old books. On the wall above one of the tables, a huge whiteboard stretched out, with notes scrawled in black and red ink. Still more papers hung with magnets.

"All that's missing is the red string, and this would be straight out of an episode of *Homeland*," Orion muttered, drawing the orb of light closer as he investigated. "Looks like most of it is in some other language, although I don't recognize it."

I didn't either, but then, that was probably a good thing. If Linda was planning to cast a blood magic spell, it likely meant the words were written in the language of the Nevermore, something of a code used by dark arts practitioners to conceal their spells.

The whole room gave me a spooky feeling. "Come on," I said, moving for the door. "The women are down here somewhere."

Orion hung back a moment, still studying the notes and papers on the board. His expression was intense as he tried to make sense of it all.

"Orion!" I hissed, gesturing for him to follow me.

Blinking, he pulled back and shook his head. "Right," he replied, following me closely into the room beyond. It was a large open room, with two doors leading out onto the back patio. A few boxes stood stacked along the wall and a large ornate rug was spread across the wood floor, but beyond that, the room was bare. I imagined it had been built to serve as a family room, or a den. A casual gathering place for the family who lived in the home. However, it appeared Linda was using it as more of a storage area. I wanted to open some of the boxes and see if there were more items relating back to the world of forbidden magic, but I resisted, and lifted my flashlight to shine it at the three doors on the other side. The one in the middle shone with some kind of ward when I hit with the light, more strange letters and runes glowing red under the fire's glow.

"Orion, look." I pointed. "Do you know what any of that means?"

His expression went steely. Without answering, he muttered another incantation and held his hands out toward the ward. Tension built between his brows as he concentrated on the magic.

My lungs began to burn and I realized I was holding my breath.

After what seemed like an hour, but was likely only a few minutes, Orion grunted one final word and the ward exploded in a blinding flash of light.

I stared at him, blinking to clear the fuzzy spots from my vision, then followed him into the room beyond. The space was bare-bones, much like the greater room on the other side of the wall. Four camping-style cots sat in the four corners, each one occupied. The blankets each had a pretty floral print, and a sick surge went through me, thinking about Linda, in her little tracksuit, wandering through a Bed Bath & Beyond, picking out bedding for her soon-to-be victims.

A whimpered sob came from one of the beds, and Orion turned, quickly lowering the flame ball when it hit Peyton square in the face.

"Peyton!" I almost yelped, rushing to her side.

She blinked. "Rosella? What are you—" Her expression changed, her eyes growing wide. "Not you, too!"

"Huh?"

"You're not like her, are you?" Peyton said, her voice growing louder.

"Shh!" I covered her mouth with my hand for a moment, my pulse spiking. "No. No. I'm not. I'm here to help."

"The window has some markings," Orion noted, taking another step into the room. "I don't think I can break this spell. The last one took a lot out of me. Wards aren't my specialty."

The others started to stir. Orion allowed the orb of light to brighten a hair, illuminating the room. Olivia, Amber, and Krystal all stared at us, confused and distraught. "Who are you?" Amber asked.

Orion held out a hand. "There's time for that later. For now, we have to get out of here. We're going to get you to safety."

"Come on," I said, offering my hand to Peyton. "We have to go, now."

The other three women exchanged a glance, as though they weren't sure whether they could trust us or not. I supposed it was understandable. Mother only knew what mind games Linda had played with them over the past months. They looked to Peyton, who had taken my hand and allowed me to help her from the cot.

"They're the good guys," she whispered to the others. "He's with Warden Quinton."

Quiet excitement rippled through them and Orion pleaded with them to keep quiet. "We need to get moving," he said.

"This way," I told Peyton, still clinging to her hand.

We turned toward the darkened doorway, and then, out of the darkness, another voice rose above the flurry of whispered plans, and a light burst on overhead. Linda stood in the doorway, a wand in her hand. Scowling, she pointed it at me. "Not so fast."

CHAPTER EIGHTEEN

*W*ithout hesitation, Orion threw himself between me and Linda, his broad shoulders concealing me and the other four women in the room. With a guttural word, he ignited two flames, one dancing in each palm. The right was blue, the left red. "You *really* don't want to try anything, lady," he growled.

"Don't I?" Linda spat back, the tip of her wand glowing a menacing green. "You broke into my house!"

"Is your brain broken?" I exclaimed. "You were *kidnapping* people! We're not here to raid your jewelry box or steal your TV!"

The flames in Orion's hands shifted, melting and dripping over the sides of his hands, until they hung like flame-coated tendrils. It took a moment to realize what was happening, but the flames somehow morphed into weapons. The blue flames expanded, forming a round shield, which he raised to chest height. While the red flame burned even brighter as it stretched toward the floor, creating a linked chain, leading to a spiked ball of flames, like a supernatural morning-star.

If I were Linda, that would have been the moment where I wet my pants.

Instead, she flicked out with a green whip of magic. Orion held the shield up, absorbing the blow of magic. I jumped back, blocking Peyton and the others as best as I could. One of them bashed on the window in a desperate attempt to get free, but Linda's enchantment held and the woman was drawn back with a hiss of pain as the magic bit into her fists where she'd punched into the spell.

Orion swung the morning-star—not an ideal weapon for such close quarters—and managed to knock the wand from Linda's hands. I took a prema-ture breath of relief, only for her to fan out her hands and send a gale of icy wind at us. The flames of Orion's weapons sputtered under the force of it and my heart sank.

My own powers were worthless, unless there was a hungry lion nearby that I could coax into turning the evil witch into a midnight snack. Which I seriously doubted. Glancing behind me, I considered the four women. They all had to have magic. One of each element. Peyton, seeming to read my desperate thought, squared her shoulders and stood beside me.

With a similar spell to the one Orion used, a ball of flames danced to life on the palm of her hand. Her flame was purple, so dark it was almost blue in the center. She didn't seem capable of turning it into a weapon, the way Orion had, but she flung out her hand and released the flame toward Linda.

Linda dodged the purple flame, and it provided the split-second distraction Orion needed. He lunged forward, the flames shifting as he moved, so fast it was almost impossible to see the change before it was done. The flames glowed red hot, then died, and for a panic-stricken moment, I thought his magic had failed, only to realize it had simply changed again, this time forming a knotted loop around Linda's hands.

Linda shrieked as she was snared, then called forth another spell, this one in a language I'd never heard. A pressure rose through the room, as though she were physically calling particles of matter to do her bidding. The back of my neck tingled with the sensation of the dark magic, though I could not see it for myself.

Blood magic.

"No!" I screamed, throwing myself toward her, desperate to stop her before she reached the end of the incantation.

That's when Amber joined the fray. With a toss of her own magic—earth—Linda's lips were sealed by a giant leaf that Amber appeared to have plucked from the houseplant in the far corner of the room.

Linda's eyes went wide as the plant adhered to her

face, forming an almost suction-cup-like hold. She tried to speak—to scream—but it came out muffled and unintelligible. The magic power she'd been calling forth vanished in a whispered *whoosh*, like the pressure seal on a bottled drink being broken.

Orion marched Linda into the other room and I found the light switch. He pulled a chair in from the other room and secured Linda to it and replaced the magic cord he'd conjured with a zip tie, cinching it tight.

"Is everyone okay?" I asked, checking each of the four women.

They all assured me they were.

"How did you even know where to find us?" Peyton asked me.

My eyes narrowed as I shot a look at Linda. She'd stopped struggling, but the hatred in her eyes had only grown. "Fluffy told me all about your twisted plans."

Her brows lifted and a muffled squeak came from behind the leaf gag. It sounded like *Mruphhy*.

That part seemed to hurt her the most, that the small dog she'd confided in all this time was the one to betray her.

"So, it's true what they say about you?" Peyton said, glancing at me, then the other women. "You can ... control other beings?"

Orion came to stand beside me. "Rosella's powers saved your lives. This crackpot was set to kill all of you in two days, on the full moon." He cast a scowl over his shoulder at Linda, before adding, "She fancies herself a blood mage, and thought she could spill yours to bring her daughter back from the dead."

I blinked. "What?"

Orion rubbed his jaw, as though he hadn't meant to reveal so much. "I saw it, there in her scribblings."

"She thought she could raise someone from the dead? But that's ... that's—"

"Nuts? Yeah, agreed." Orion grabbed his phone from his pocket and excused himself from the room.

"Thank you, Rosella," Peyton said. "I—I didn't mean any offense. I was just surprised. I mean, when you came back, people ... well—" She broke off, looking a little embarrassed.

"I know," I told her. "Some of the rumors are true. I *can* communicate with animals, and in the right circumstances, I can even see the world through their eyes. It doesn't work on humans. I can't climb inside anyone's head and take over the power steering."

The four women looked relieved. I knew it wasn't personal, it was more the idea of that level of power even existing in the world that upset them, but it was hard not to take it to heart. I didn't want anyone to be afraid of me.

Okay, well, maybe people like Linda, but certainly not other people in town.

All I could hope was that when word about what transpired under Linda's roof got out, it would paint me in a slightly more favorable light. Hey, maybe there was hope for one day coming home and finding a town of people happy to see me instead of shrinking back in fear of the unknown, or lashing out with crazy accusations, like the woman at town hall.

It wouldn't be enough to make me want to stay. It was too little, too late. But it would be a welcome change of pace next time I came home for the holidays.

IN THE END, whether he deserved it or not, it was Sheriff Templeton who got credit for making the arrest that officially ended the case of the missing joggers. Linda was carted out of her home by four deputies and the sheriff himself. The women were all taken directly to see a healer, though they all insisted they were fine. As Fluffy had said, Linda had kept them in good condition, at least on the outside. On the inside ... well, the four would likely require months, if not years, of working through the trauma of their ordeal and rebuild their lives.

When the scene was cleared, Sheriff Templeton circled back around to me and Orion, his expression grim. "What you did tonight was rash and irresponsible, Ms. Midnight. You could have gotten yourself killed, not to mention further endanger these women's lives."

"And here I was, thinking you should be offering her a key to the city for saving your hide," Orion said

gruffly. "What would the townspeople have thought when all four women ended up dead in some sick blood ritual on the full moon?"

I set a hand on his arm. I didn't need him to fight this particular battle. "I'm just happy the women are safe. This was never about some kind of hunt for glory."

The sheriff's lip curled back, but he kept his mouth closed, opting instead for a brief nod. "I'll need to see you both at the station, to give an official statement of the events that transpired here. Do you need a ride?"

"My truck is across the street," Orion answered, placing one hand at the small of my back to lead me away from the sneering sheriff. "Even after all that, he can't find an ounce of humility," he muttered as we walked out the doors into the backyard of Linda's home.

I shivered as the sweat on my brow rapidly evaporated in the freezing temperature. Orion stopped and took ahold of my arms. "You okay? That was a lot to process."

"I—I'm fine," I stammered.

"It's okay to *not* be okay. You know that, right?" A hint of a smile tugged at his lips and for one insane moment, I wanted to throw myself against his chest and ignore everything else while I caught my breath.

My mind was whirling too fast, the thoughts dancing in and out so quickly I couldn't fully track any of them. Some were glimpses of what would have happened if we hadn't shown up tonight. Others were of the way Orion had moved during the peak of the fight. Flashes of his flamed weapons. The look of terror in the women's eyes when they realized what their fate was to be.

"Come on," Orion said, interrupting the wild kaleidoscope of chaos. "Let's get into the truck where it's warm. We fire mages can be a little pitiful in the cold." He grinned at me.

"Pitiful?" I laughed. There was no way—under any circumstances—I could associate that word with the man walking beside me.

Orion chuckled and led the way to the truck. He fired up the engine and it didn't take long for warm air to blast through the vents. We hadn't been in Linda's house more than half an hour. Everything had happened so fast.

Fluffy was pressed up against the back passenger window, his panting breaths leaving little foggy circles on the glass.

"You'd better not be getting a bunch of noseprints on my windows," Orion told the dog, a teasing glint in his eyes.

"What happened? Where are they taking her?" the little dog asked, launching himself back over the center console to bury himself under my arm.

"She's going away for a long, long time," I told Fluffy, stroking his fur in an attempt to calm his frantic breathing.

Glancing up at Orion, I smiled. "Speaking of, you interested in giving this little guy a forever home?"

Laughing, he pulled out onto the road and pulled a U-turn in the middle of the street. "Maybe if he was a Doberman."

Fluffy looked up and scowled. *"Hey!"*

Smiling, I smoothed the dog's fur. "Don't feel bad. You wouldn't want to go live with him anyway," I told him. "He's always crawling around in bushes and climbing trees, probably goes weeks without showering."

Orion cut a sidelong glance at me, still grinning. "We talking about me or the dog?"

"Definitely you," I replied, smiling as some of the heaviness in my chest lifted.

Heaving one shoulder, Orion sighed. "I guess I can't argue. I do make a pretty terrible roommate."

"Think you'll ever settle down?" I asked.

"Rosella, I'm not taking the dog," he replied.

I rolled my eyes. "That's not why I was asking."

Flashing that wicked smile, he looked at me. "Oh? Well, then why were you asking? You looking for a *roommate?*"

"You're impossible," I scoffed, desperately ignoring the little flutter in my stomach.

At least, mostly.

CHAPTER NINETEEN

"*H*ave you lost your senses?"

To say that my family was taken aback by my midnight adventures would be a massive understatement. Gathered in the kitchen the following morning, my mom wore the look she used to give right before grounding me for a week. Dad was more shocked into silence, worry lines showing between his brows, as if he were trying to decide if I'd been temporarily abducted by aliens and had my brain rewired.

"No," I protested, turning toward my mom. "What was I supposed to do? Let them kill an innocent creature just to have a scapegoat? It wouldn't have stopped Peyton from getting taken. And they probably would have just blamed that on Orion not acting quickly enough."

"Orion?" my father repeated, looking to my mom.

"The warden's monster slayer," she explained impatiently. "The nice young man who picked Rosella up the other night."

Dad's brows lifted another half an inch as he looked at me. "You're dating the monster hunter?"

"No!" I threw my hands in the air as Jasmine, Candice, and Grandma Rose all tittered together.

"He did have a rather nice butt," Grandma Rose interjected, with a cheery little smile.

Mom blinked, looking at her own mother. "Mom!"

Grandma Rose shrugged. "Just call them like I see them."

I scrubbed a hand down my face. "I didn't get enough sleep to deal with any of this," I muttered.

Jasmine helpfully shoved the coffee carafe toward me.

"Listen," I said, holding my hands up, "maybe it was rash, ill-advised, reckless ... whatever. At the end of the day, I was right, and I helped save four women's lives. I think that should be the main takeaway here. Don't you?"

"No!" my mother exclaimed. "You could have been killed, Rosella! You should have called the sheriff as soon as you knew something was going on in that house! That's his job, not yours."

"You're right, it is his job, but he'd already dropped that ball and kicked it into the middle of the Pacific Ocean! He had a chance to close this case; the would-be murderer has been living under his nose this entire time. Even without Valkyrie's word, it was obvious to see that this shoddy investigation he's been running was a bare-minimum effort, something to do in between occupying a stool at Merlin's Well!"

Dad frowned. "And Valkyrie is …?"

I sighed. "The sea serpent."

"Rosella!"

Shoving away from the table, I stood up. "I'm sorry to have upset you, but I made my choices and I stand by them. I'm thirty years old and I can handle myself."

Stalking from the kitchen, I paused in the hall, just out of sight, when Grandma Rose piped up in my defense. "Oh, Penelope, don't be so hard on the girl. She's been on her own now for the better part of a decade. She knows what she can handle."

My mother scoffed. "Sure, right up until some sorcerer gets ahold of her!"

"Come on, dear," my father said. I could picture him reaching for her waist, trying to draw her near before she launched into a ferocious cleaning session. Back when Jasmine and I were teenagers, they'd had to replace the kitchen sink because she managed to scrub the enamel off with a steel wool pad. "We need to take it easy on her. She just got home. We don't want to lose her again. Not like last time."

My heart twisted as I pushed away from the wall and tiptoed to my bedroom.

THE ONLY PERSON who thought it was cool was Matty. The day after the raid, the bare bones of the story appeared in a special edition of the *Winterspell Gazette* and Matty came to Sugar Shack, demanding to know why he hadn't been texted immediately after everything happened. He wasn't angry, so much as bummed he'd had to find out via the paper. He took me out to lunch and I recapped the whole fiasco, leaving out the details of Orion's magic. Prior to dropping me at home, Orion had asked me to keep some of those details a little fuzzy in the retelling. The mystery surrounding his power was apparently important to the warden and only to be revealed if absolutely necessary.

I was just wrapping up lunch with Matty, when a sheriff's deputy called and informed me that Sheriff Templeton had requested my return to the station. Assuming he wanted to rant and rave some more, I dragged my feet getting there, but when I arrived, learned that it wasn't the sheriff who wanted to speak with me.

It was Linda.

The sorceress was being held in a magic-proof cell at the station, pending transportation to her formal trial before the Arcane Wardens. One of Templeton's deputies led me to the cell and showed me the two-way communication system in place. A table sat in the middle of the cell, but the deputy assured me there was a barrier of powerful protection charms set in the middle of the room, slicing straight down the middle of the table. I would be safe from Linda, while still being able to hear and see her, as if there was nothing between us.

"You ready?" the deputy, a young female with a serious face, asked.

"Do you know what she wants from me?"

The deputy shook her head. "She hasn't said anything to us. She says she'll only talk to you."

My lips formed a hard line and I gave the deputy a single nod. "I'm ready."

The deputy moved to open the large, thick door, no doubt lined with its own layers of magic and protections. I shuffled into the all-white room and found Linda sitting on one side of the table. She wore a blue jumpsuit; her once-lustrous brown hair appeared slightly bedraggled as it hung loose around her shoulders. She looked older without the jewelry, makeup, and freshly done tresses. It was somehow easier to imagine her having had an adult daughter.

Her palms lay flat on the table's edge, her wrists bound with a glowing pulse of some spell. She glanced up when she heard the door; her green eyes were hollow, red rimming the edges from recent tears. "Rosella. You came."

Tentatively, I moved into the room, approaching the table. There was no sign of the magic protection shield. I had to trust that it was all in place, and that this wasn't some kind of setup.

Stop being so cynical.

"I'll admit," I began, pulling out the chair, "I didn't expect this."

Linda bobbed her chin. "I wanted to thank you."

"Thank me?"

"Yes." Linda sniffed. She reached up, as though to wipe her nose, only to remember her wrists were bound. Dropping her hands to her lap, she looked down for a long moment.

I didn't rush her, even as my curiosity spiked.

Finally, she cleared her throat and explained. "When my daughter, Ariana, got sick, I vowed that I would move heaven and earth to find a cure for her. And when she ... when she died, I didn't accept it. I couldn't. I knew there was a way to get her back, that someone, somewhere, would have another option. That her death didn't have to be the end." Linda paused and sniffled.

Her green eyes met mine and she continued. "I lost all of my family and friends. They thought I was crazy. Deranged. Obsessed. Whatever other things they said. I traveled all over the world, trying to find someone who could help me. And when I did, and they told me the price—what was needed to cast the spell, I walked away for a time. I tried to move on, to start new hobbies and make new friends."

"Hence the running club?" I inserted.

She nodded. "It helped, but I still missed my daughter so much, and I got all twisted up—"

Her voice broke as a fresh wave of tears welled up in her eyes. She stared past me, to some nondescript place on the wall, and shook her head. "I can't believe I've done all these terrible things. To my ... my friends."

Her body convulsed in a sob as she folded in half, burying her face in her bound hands.

I waited, unsure if there was anything I could—or should—say. The idea of abducting four women, holding them captive, all while plotting to *murder* them ... it was beyond my comprehension. How could someone justify taking four other daughters from their mothers, to bring their own child back?

"I used the club," Linda continued, her voice thick. "I used it to pick them. I needed one of each type of magic for the spell to work. I also was careful to make sure they would be people who could ... lift out easily. I picked them because they didn't have a lot going on. I knew their schedules, their lives."

I blinked. She was overcome with emotion and regret, and while it felt authentic, there was still something so cold and calculating to her words. There was one part of her explanation that made no sense. If you wanted to "disappear" four women, a small town—especially one like Winterspell—was hardly the ideal target.

Tilting my head to one side, I narrowed my eyes.

"What led you here in the first place? To Winterspell, I mean?"

Something flickered in Linda's eyes and it took me a moment to realize it was fear. She turned away, looking at the wall. "I can't say anything about that."

"Linda—"

"Please, don't ask me anymore about it. I can't tell you."

"Is there someone … or some*thing* here in Winter-spell? Something to do with … blood magic?"

Abruptly, she snapped back to look at me. "He'll kill me," she hissed, her voice low and desperate. "I'm not saying another word."

I stared at her. For as fierce as her eyes looked, there was a slight tremor to her shoulders. She was terrified. Nodding, I dropped it. "Okay."

She exhaled and sank back against her chair.

"Is there anything else, then?" I asked, my hands on the table, readying to stand.

Linda tucked her chin, staring back down at her hands.

When she didn't answer, I got up and headed toward the door.

"Wait!"

Turning back, I met her eyes and noticed a tear slipping free.

"You'll take care of Fluffy? If not for my sake, then … for my Ariana."

I nodded, making a solemn vow. "I'll make sure he finds a good home."

Linda nodded, her lower lip trembling. "Thank you."

Without another word, I left the room, and the deputy shut the heavy door with a resolute *thump*, sealing Linda in her prison, though as I left the station, I wondered which was worse, the physical prison she was trapped inside, or the one she'd built herself out of grief.

WANDERING THROUGH TOWN, a new restlessness began building within me. It took me some time, but when I realized what was nagging at me, I knew what I needed to do. There was one final piece of the puzzle I needed to set right.

To say Rick Shaver wasn't happy to see me would be an understatement. "What are *you* doing here?" he asked, barring me entrance into his studio by squaring off his shoulders, crossing his arms, and planting his legs wide over the threshold. "Do you have more wild accusations to throw at me?"

"No," I replied, shaking my head. "I'm here to apologize."

Rick's brows lifted and he dropped his arms to his sides.

"I didn't have the right to come here and sling

around those ugly accusations. I won't make any excuses; there aren't any. If anyone should know what it feels like to be accused to ugly things, it's me, and yet, I did it to you without thinking. And for that, I am deeply sorry. I hope you can accept my apology."

Rick inclined his chin, thinking it through. "Is it true, what the paper said? That you led the rescue mission that saved Olivia, Krystal, Amber, and Peyton?"

I nodded. "I got lucky. Right place, right time, I guess."

A small smile ghosted across his lips. "I'd say it was more than luck."

"I'm just glad everyone is safe."

"I am, too." Rick scrubbed a hand over his stubbled jawline. "Those women are more than clients, like I said. When you work together on something like fitness, it's easy to become friends. Reading the news that they were all safe this morning ... well, it was a big relief. So, for your part in all of it, whatever it was, thank you."

I didn't know what to say, so I just bobbed my head, then turned to leave.

I'd gone a few steps when Rick called out for me, "Rosella, wait."

"Hmm?"

Rick had slipped his hands into the pockets of his workout shorts. "If you ever want to come in for training, your first session is on me, okay?"

I blinked. "You'd take me on as a client, after the things I said?"

Rick shrugged. "You owned up to it, and I respect that. We all make boneheaded mistakes sometimes, right?" He smiled. "You're welcome in my gym, anytime."

"Thanks, Rick. I just might take you up on that offer."

"Good." He held up one hand. "See you around."

I returned his wave. "See you."

CHAPTER TWENTY

*O*rion came to the house just before dusk on Wednesday. He knocked on the front door of my parents' house and asked my mom if he could see me. The whole thing felt very high school, especially considering the argument we'd all had around the breakfast table that morning. Thankfully, Grandma Rose was taking a pre-dinner nap and wasn't in the front room to ogle him. Jasmine and Candice were at Sugar Shack and also unavailable to comment.

I hustled him out onto the porch and closed the front door behind me.

Orion grinned. "You hiding me from them?"

"If I say *yes* can we go walk down by the lake?"

He chuckled and nodded. "All right, but for the record, I'm very good with parents."

Narrowing my eyes, I considered him. "This isn't a date."

"I know."

"Are you sure, because you seem to keep getting confused."

He laughed as he jogged down the front steps. "Actually, I have something to show you. So, hop in." He gestured toward his truck.

I caught him up on the conversation with Linda as we drove through town. "The weirdest part was when I asked her about what drew her to Winterspell in the first place. I mean, she had been saying she'd done all this traveling, to try and find someone to help her, and then she pivoted and made it sound like she'd found that answer here ... in Winterspell."

Orion glanced at me. "Did you ask her?"

"Yeah, and she got kind of ... weird." The memory of her haunted, half-crazed eyes flashed through my mind, and I shook my head. "She said *he* would kill her, if she talked about it."

"He who?" Orion asked.

"I have no idea ..."

"Well, good thing that's not foreboding or anything," he replied.

"I don't know what to make of it," I said, ignoring his heavy sarcasm. "Does that mean that whoever taught her those spells is from around here?"

Orion went quiet.

"Orion?" I prompted, twisting in my seat to face his profile. "What do you know? How did you know what all those blood magic spells would do, if she'd followed through on them?"

A muscle flexed in his jaw. "Nothing I can tell you about. At least, not now."

"Why not?"

"Because, it could be dangerous," he said, before turning on the charm again.

"And you know, you're a little bit of a loose cannon. Breaking into people's houses in the middle of the night and all that." He flashed me a quick wink.

I punched his bicep—which was rock hard and probably hurt my knuckles more than his arm.

"You sound like my mother," I complained, shaking out my fist.

He chuckled, then pointed out the windshield. "Here we are."

"A motel?"

He drove around the side of the two-story motel. It was far from fancy, but the exterior looked clean and well-maintained. In the back lot, Orion pulled his truck beside a larger box truck. "Come on," he said, already halfway out the door.

I followed him to the back of the box truck and he lifted the garage-style door to reveal a huge glass tank.

Two familiar eyes glowed from the shadows.

"Valkyrie!" I gasped.

The sea serpent propelled herself to the front of the huge tank and I finally got a look at the rest of her body. She wasn't quite as large as I'd expected, her head almost disproportionally large by comparison. Her long body was covered in the iridescent scales I'd seen along her neck, making her entire body change color and shade based on the light. She did in fact have short legs, or … arms? Tucked up along her body. They looked more like flippers than anything else.

"We're about to head out on a little road trip," Orion said, tapping the glass with the pads of his fingertips.

"Where are you taking her?"

"Someplace where she can live free," he answered, giving the serpent a reverent glance before returning his eyes to mine. "She's not safe here in Winterspell anymore. Someone will try to hunt her; whether for trophy or out of a sense of protection, they will kill her."

Orion latched a clip on the side of his toolbox, heaved it into the back of his truck, and then pulled the hatch down and locked it. "I know a good spot out in Oregon. There aren't any people around, other than the occasional campers or hikers, so it won't be hard for her to live in peace, without fear of capture. By this time tomorrow, she'll be all settled into her new home."

I didn't know why, but the description made my eyes well up. "Thank you, Orion."

He grinned. "What's it going to take to get you to call me Ryan?"

I laughed. "Right, right. Sorry. Thank you, Ryan."

"You're welcome, Rosella."

DANIELLE GARRETT

"You can call me Ella," I told him, with a little shrug. "If you want to. It's what my friends call me."

"Friends?" His brows rose as his smile widened, that dimpled cleft making an appearance.

I shoved his arm. "Yes! Friends. Now, don't make me regret it."

He laughed and opened his arms. "Come here."

We embraced, the feeling almost odd in that it felt like we were longtime friends. But then, considering everything we'd gone through in the past few days, maybe it wasn't so weird after all.

Stepping out of the hug, I moved to Valkyrie's temporary cage, and placed my hand upon the thick glass wall. "You're okay," I told her. "You'll be safe."

The majestic creature blinked slowly. *"Thank you, Rosella. I will go and be at peace."*

Orion looked at me expectantly.

"She said she's at peace."

He smiled. "Good."

He let me linger a moment longer, then moved to close the huge door on the truck.

"What's next for you? Something dangerous, I'm sure," I said, stepping back to let him work.

He cast me a carefree grin. "That's the way I like it."

"You're an adrenaline junkie," I teased.

"Pot, meet kettle," he tossed back with a wink. "I've never been trapped inside a creepy murder house before I met you."

"An *almost* murder house," I corrected, as if somehow that made it better.

"Right." Orion laughed. "I'll say it again, Ella, you'd make one heck of an agent, if you ever get bored around here."

"Maybe," I said, though it wasn't a serious consideration. Working for the agency was the last thing I wanted to do. I was trying to get away from magic, not dive down into the thickest parts of it.

"Either way, I have a feeling this isn't the last we'll be seeing of each other," he said, stepping back. He slid his hands into his pockets, his expression going serious as he looked off toward the mountains surrounding the lake. "I have questions that need answers, Ella. And I might need your help in getting them."

I tilted my head, not quite sure what he meant. "That's kind of cryptic."

He took my arms and held me still. "Just keep your eyes open, all right?"

I nodded, a swoop of anxiety cutting through my stomach. "I will."

DESPITE THE RUCKUS the morning after Linda's arrest, things at my parents' house settled quickly and I worked to adjust to my new routine. I worked at Sugar Shack as many shifts as I could, hoping to sock away as much money as possible, so that when the time came,

I'd have a solid foundation to build upon. Jake called me the following Tuesday, letting me know my car was fixed and ready for pickup.

We hadn't spoken since the night at Merlin's Well, and as much as I wanted my wheels back, the idea of going to his shop—and seeing the new life he'd created for himself—was not something I wanted to face. In the end, I had no choice. There was paperwork that needed my final signature, and I couldn't send Jasmine or my dad to do it for me.

I walked into Jake's shop Tuesday afternoon, my hands in my pockets, as if I were strolling through a shop selling pricey breakables and didn't trust myself to not reach out and touch things.

He greeted me at the counter, wearing a pair of black-framed glasses.

"Those are new," I said, gesturing at my own eyes.

"Oh." He chuckled and removed them, tucking them into the pocket on his clean work shirt. "Getting up there, I guess."

I laughed. "Don't say that, because if you're getting older, then it means I am, too."

He smiled a moment longer, then plucked a pair of keys from a rack behind the counter. "I believe these belong to you. I like the keychain from Hawaii. When did you go over there?"

"Oh. Well, I haven't, yet." I ran a finger over the rose gold palm tree dangling from a silver ring. "I got this as kind of an inspiration thing, I guess."

"Aha. Well, you'll get there. I have no doubts."

The printer behind him whirred to life and spat out a small stack of papers. "That will be the final documentation for the insurance company. Just a couple of signatures and I'll get you on your way."

"Thanks."

My phone rang and I automatically reached for it. The number that popped up wasn't one I recognized, but it was a Portland area code.

"I need to take this," I told Jake, already moving away from the counter.

"No problem," he replied.

Answering the call, I cleared my throat. "Hello?"

"Hello. Is this Rosella Midnight?" a woman asked.

"This is her." I arched a brow. "May I ask who's calling?"

Probably someone trying to sell me a time-share.

"Of course," the woman replied gracefully. "My name is Cheryl Hyde. I'm the hiring manager for the *Rose City Rambler*."

My heart shot up like a champagne cork. "Oh! Hi!"

Cheryl laughed softly. "Is this a good time? I'd like to speak with you about the resume you submitted two weeks ago."

The *Rose City Rambler* was an independent publication, mostly based online, with a heavy emphasis on the moves of the upwardly mobile. I'd submitted my resume right after losing my job. Working for a glorified gossip magazine wasn't my dream job, but hobnobbing with the rich and powerful was bound to uncover a juicy story sooner or later—one I could then pitch to a real news outlet in exchange for a byline, and maybe have a shot at moving past the nasty plagiarism accusations that currently marred my resume.

The plan had all made sense in my head when I'd applied, but in hindsight, it felt stupid and shallow. Turning back, I found Jake watching me. He quickly looked back at his computer screen, and I smiled to myself.

Some unexplainable emotion rose through me and I knew what I needed to do. "Cheryl, I really appreciate the call, but I think I'm going to have to pass. I was given another opportunity, and I think I need to see where it goes."

Cheryl spouted some polite well-wishes and we ended the call.

Walking back to the counter, Jake looked up again. "All set?"

Nodding, I smiled. "I think so."

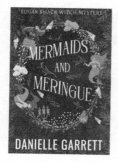

It's New Year's Eve and Rosella Midnight has a date with danger.

A handsome date for New Year's Eve? Check.

Red lipstick and a killer party dress? Double check.

A kiss when the clock strikes twelve? Undecided.

If I'm going to be stuck in Winterspell a little longer, I may as well have fun with it. But you know what they say about the best laid plans...

When my romantic evening turns into a kidnapping investigation, I can't wait around to watch the ball drop. There's a mermaid-snatching monster on the loose, and it's up to me to stop them.

Luckily for me, my date always comes loaded for dragon.

Get your copy of Mermaids and Meringue and return to Winterspell today!

And in case you missed it, there is a holiday-themed novella set between the events of Sprinkles and Sea Serpents and Mermaids and Meringue. Check out *Grimoires and Gingerbread* for a Christmas adventure in Winterspell!

. . .

SIGN up for my newsletter to make sure you're the first to know when I have a new release, promotion, or fun freebies! You get two prequels just for joining, so head over to my website to get signed up now.

www.DanielleGarrettBooks.com/newsletter

IF YOU CAN'T GET enough Winterspell fun and want to chat about it with other readers, come join the Bat Wings Book Club on Facebook. It's my happy little corner of the internet and I love chatting with readers and sharing behind the scenes fun.

UNTIL NEXT TIME, **happy reading!**
  Danielle Garrett
  www.DanielleGarrettBooks.com

MAGIC AND MYSTERY AWAIT IN BEECHWOOD HARBOR

One town. Two spunky leading ladies.
More magic than you can shake a wand at.
Welcome to Beechwood Harbor.

Come join the fun in Beechwood Harbor, the little town where witches, shifters, ghosts, and vamps all live, work, play, and— mostly—get along!

The two main series set in this world are the Beechwood Harbor Magic Mysteries and the Beechwood Harbor Ghost Mysteries.

In the following pages you will find more information about those books, as well as my other works available.

Alternatively, you can find a complete reading list on my website:

www.DanielleGarrettBooks.com

ABOUT THE AUTHOR

As a lifelong bookworm, Danielle Garrett has always loved dreaming of fantastic places and the stories they have to share. Through her love of reading, she's followed along on hundreds of adventures through the eyes of wizards, princesses, elves, and some rather wonderful everyday people as well. This lifelong passion led her into the world of writing and she has now achieved the dream she's held since the second grade and become an author herself.

Danielle lives in Oregon, and while she travels as often as possible, she wouldn't call anywhere else home. She shares her life with her husband and their house full of animals. When she's not writing, she can be found serving as the dedicated servant to three extremely spoiled cats or chasing down the most recent item the puppy has turned into a chew toy.

Visit Danielle today at her website or say "hello" on Facebook.

www.DanielleGarrettBooks.com

Made in the USA
Monee, IL
26 June 2025

20079149R00177